Tiger's Blood

Elizabeth Morris

ISBN:1539327019
ISBN-13: 978-1539327011

DEDICATION

I would like to dedicate this to my mom, Jennifer Keeler, who supported me throughout my writing process, and to myself for actually getting this book done.

CONTENTS

Tiger's Blood

ACKNOWLEDGMENTS

I would like to thank Ashley Babcock who helped me edit my work. Thank you to all of my close friends who inspired me to create certain characters. Thank you to Mike who pushed me to finish and publish my book. Thank you to my cat Puff for inspiring the design of Kira. Thank you everyone for all the support and excitement throughout this process.

PROLOGUE

The rough winds glide our boat swiftly throughout the sapphire sea. I look ahead at the green land in the distance and I sigh. *A year of traveling on this smelly sea and we finally get here. If the weather wasn't so horrible we would have gotten here sooner.* I turn around and watch the hundreds of boats with the gold and red symbol of the Lions on the sails following behind me and I smile. *My Kingdom of the Lions. I'm glad that so many Bloods decided to follow me.* "Bryce!" I yell loudly. My young servant quickly scurries through the ship to get to me. "Yes sir?" he asks. "Please bring me my sons at once," I look in his anxious, brown eyes and he nods. "Yes, of course, your highness," he says. *Your highness, I can get used to that. This was a great idea leaving that shithole home behind.*

Bryce comes back with my eldest son Jett and I frown at him. "Are you deaf? I told you to bring *both* of my sons," I say angrily. "Yes sir but-but Ethan, he won't leave his room," he stutters. "He won't stop crying daddy, it's starting to get really annoying," Jett tells me. "Ugh, alright I'll go get him myself," I grunt. Jett follows behind me as we push through the crowd.
The crew bows their heads as my son and I walk by. We stop at my stateroom and I walk inside. I eye my youngest son squalling in his bed, red faced and miserable.
I walk over and sit next to him on his bed. He looks up at me with his light grey eyes and I frown. "What is all your fussing about Ethan? People are complaining," I ask. He wipes his big eyes and little nose and looks down at the ground. "I-I want mommy. When is mommy coming back?" he sniffles. I roll my eyes and stand up in front of him and sigh loudly. "How many times do I have to tell you that your mother is dead boy. Her body burned up in an immense fire. She is never coming back. Your brother got over it so why can't you?" I yell. He starts bawling again and I groan in anger. "Bryce!" I yell again. He shuffles in the room quickly. "Yes, King Andrew?" he says. "Calm down

my toddler and when he stops crying bring him to me. He needs to get over this sooner or later. Preferably sooner," I say. "Yes sir," he says and Jett and I leave the room.

I walk back to the helm of the boat and look back out towards the land. I turn around to the captain. "How much longer until we reach that land?" I ask. "No more than an hour sir. Do you know where we will settle all of the Lions?" he asks me. "We will make camp just off the coast for now. I'll go talk to my top builders to design our future Kingdom," I say. The captain nods and I leave him. I walk to the promenade deck and take a seat in a cold, metal chair. I snap my fingers; a servant comes over and stands in front of me.

"Yes, King Andrew?" he says. "Fetch me Alan, Basil, and Glenn please, I need to discuss the plans for the Kingdom. Also, go to the galley and ask them to cook me something other than disgusting fish. I'm tired of seafood," I say. "Right away sir," he says and leaves. Moments later, the designers show up and sit down at the table. "Hello your highness, how are you doing?" Alan asks. "Fine, fine, I need to ask you three a question," I say. "Anything your highness," Glenn says.

"I need you to design me a rough draft of a Kingdom to build, but I want to make sure that no one will disturb my Lions. I don't want any other Bloods besides Lions in my Kingdom. If there are others who would like to be in the Kingdom, then they will be servants. Of course, they won't be treated the same as the Lions. We are more superior than any other Blood in Bitotem and I want everyone to know it," I say. "So what you are saying is that you want a large Kingdom that is hidden from other Bloods?" Alan asks. He taps Basil on the shoulder and he starts sketching on a large white paper.

"Yes, I want a hidden Kingdom. Will that be a problem?" I ask. Alan and Glenn look at each other nervously. "Maybe, depends on what you mean by hidden sir. Do you mean you want the Kingdom *physically* hidden?" Alan asks. "Yes," I say. "I think I have an idea sir," Basil blurts out. "What's your idea?" I ask. "What if we built the Kingdom underground?" he says. Alan and Glenn laugh. "Come on Basil, be serious about this. King Andrew needs a real idea for a Kingdom," Glenn says. "Quiet, I want to hear what he has to say," I say curiously. Glenn and Alan stop laughing.

"Thank you sir. What I was saying is that I heard that Eastern Bitotem has beautiful caverns with rivers that run underground. If that is true, then we can build a Kingdom underneath the caverns. We can still get enough sunlight through, and it will be hidden from other Bloods. The only way into the Kingdom will be down," Basil says. I rub my chin with my hand and study Basil. "And what if there aren't caverns?" I ask. "If there aren't caverns, then we can build it above ground, and build a giant wall protecting the Kingdom," he says. I breathe softly. "I like it. Start sketching buildings. I want that underground Kingdom and if there are caverns over there, can you build a giant wall underground?" I ask. "Yes sir it is possible. I will get to work right away," Basil stands up and shakes my hand firmly then leaves. Alan and Glenn leave soon afterwards.

Two servants bring out white cheese, red grapes, and a glass of red wine. I pop a few grapes in my mouth when seven-year-old Jett comes by and sits next to me. "Daddy, I have a question," he says. "What is it son?" I ask. "I know you told me before, but I forgot. Why did we leave home again?" he asks. I take a sip of wine and I sit up in my chair and look him in the eye. "We left home because the Bloods who lived there were bloody idiots. They all talked about peace, equality, and fairness for all. If everyone is equal and in peace, then they form their own opinions, which will cause arguments that will lead to war. Everyone should be under the rule of a King like me to keep the order straight and keep everyone in line. Everyone will love me as King, and you in the future my son."

"Right, and what's a Blood again?" he asks. "*We* are Bloods son. We are half animal and half human. We can mutate or shift into our animal forms whenever we want to. I'm a Lion Blood, you've seen that before back home. I forgot how Bloods came to be in Bitotem, but our Blood is who we are; it is our personalities. You haven't discovered your Blood yet because you are too young, but I bet you'll be a Lion just like me," I say. Jett nods then frowns. "What's the matter Jett?" I ask. "I can't ask. You'll get upset at me," he says. *It's about Lynn I know it. I can tell by his expression.* "Is it about your mother?" I groan. He nods. "I just want to know why you killed her and the rest of the

9

village back home. Wasn't mom a Lion too? The Lions are the good guys right?" he asks.

"Yes, your mother was a Lion, but we didn't agree on things all the time. She wanted peace like those other Bloods back home. She didn't like my idea of the Kingdom. She was a selfish, good-hearted bitch," I grumble. Jett looks at me baffled. "What's a bitch daddy?" Jett asks. "You'll learn about that later. You're not old enough. Don't go repeating that around or that will make me look bad," I say and take another sip of wine. Jett takes a few bites of the cheese. "Why do you hate Ethan so much?" Jett asks. I look into his light brown eyes. *Because he acts like your stupid mother. He even has her grey eyes and her light brown hair. At least Jett looks like me and isn't dumb.* "I don't hate your brother, Jett, but he just doesn't know about this world yet. You still have a lot to learn as well."

"What do I have to learn?" he asks. "You're full of questions today aren't you?" I laugh. "Sorry, I won't ask any more questions," he lowers his head in shame. "That's alright. I was the same way when I was your age. I wanted to know everything about the world. You will learn how to become a proper King like me so that when I pass on to the next life, you and your future sons will be as great as me and my father before me. I will teach you how to fight and defend yourself. I will teach you the ways of war if there is ever such an event in the future. I will teach you right from wrong in this world," I say.

Jett looks up at me and smiles. "I want to be a Lion just like you. I want to be the best King ever," he laughs. "I bet you will be son," I smile back at him. "What about Ethan? Will he be King too?" he asks. I frown. "No. Ethan's your younger brother. After you, it will be your sons. Ethan won't really get anything. Unless you and I die before you have kids, Ethan will not have any rights to the Kingdom," I say. "Oh ok, I get it. Only the older Prince gets ownership of the Kingdom," Jett says. "Very good son," I nod at him and frown. *If somehow Jett and I die, and Ethan becomes King then this world will go to shit. He will never be allowed to be King even if I have to die for it.*

I finish my wine and walk to the bow of the boat with Jett. I look off to the land and stroke Jett's thick black hair, same as mine. *Jett will be a good King, I know it. He's just like me.* "King Andrew, sir, we should be arriving ashore in about five minutes," the captain yells behind me. "Thank you captain," I yell back at him. Bryce walks up to me with little Ethan in his long arms. Ethan rubs his eyes and sniffles lightly. "I got him to stop crying sir. Would you like to hold him?" he asks. I scowl. "No just put him next to his brother. Thank you Bryce," I say. He nods then places Ethan on the ground next to Jett.

We land ashore and I take the boys out first before the crew steps off. The moist yellow sand leaves footprints as we walk along the beach. I look off into the distance and see miles and miles of forest. *I wonder if there are any Bloods living here already in this part of Bitotem. If there are, they will follow me as their King whether they like it or not. If I have to send my men to kidnap them, then I will. I won't be shut down by Bloods who think they are better than the Lions. We are the strongest and most populated Blood in all of Bitotem. If anyone tells me I am wrong, I'll kill them. I am not getting treated like we were back home.*

"Dad, are we going to live here forever?" Jett asks me. "Yes, I already made plans to build us a Kingdom here. I will give you anything you want my son. We will live better here than back at our old home," I tell him. "Awesome, thank you for bringing me here," Jett smiles then picks up a stick and whacks it against a tree. "I'm going to be a knight!" he screams with joy. I look down and glare at Ethan who is curled up around my leg. "Daddy?" Ethan looks up at me. "Yes?" I reply. "Do you wove me?" he asks. I gulp nervously. *I despise looking into those grey eyes.* "Yes, yes. Of course," I say and give him a half smile and pat his little head. He smiles back at me and runs off to play with Jett. Ethan picks up a stick and they play together along the shore. *This child is going to be the death of me, I swear.*

1 KIRA

You really don't see it at first, but your life does flash by. I mean just look at me, 12 years of my life and it is all a blur. My mother died months after my little sister Lily was born. My mom was very wise, well to a four-year old she seemed wise. When Lily was born, she had many issues. She came out very quiet and frail. When she tried to scream or cry, no sound came out of her mouth. The doctors told me they have never seen someone with Lily's condition. Mom and dad still loved Lily no matter what she was like, and it seemed like they loved her more than me. Mother was an Owl Blood before she died.

In our world, Bitotem, everyone has a special Blood that they discover in a time in their life. Bloods are mutants, half animal half humans. We can mutate into our specific animal Blood whenever we feel that it is necessary. We mainly use our Bloods for hunting and traveling. No one knows where Bloods came from or what happened to normal humans some say we just evolved into these forms ourselves. Bloods have been in the world for centuries now. Your Blood is based off of your personality. When you discover your Blood, you have to learn how to use it and control it. Normally you discover your Blood between the ages of 16 and 20. It is rare if you discover your Blood before 16, extremely rare.

My dad is a Bear Blood; he has some anger problems. Ever since mom died, he has never been the same. He always has an eye on little Lily.

"Kira, get down here!!! Where is Lily's medicine?!?!?" He yells angrily.

I run quickly down the stairs and I hand him the small white bottle.

"Kira that is the third time I asked you, why didn't you listen to me the first time?" He looks at me with disappointment in his eyes.

"I'm sorry I just overslept. I haven't been feeling well lately," I tell him. "Well your sister is more important. She could be gone any day now," he says then places Lily's medicine on the counter.

He looks around the room and Lily starts coughing. "You give Lily her medicine then put her down for a nap. I'm going to the market to get more food or I'll hunt. Whatever's faster," he grabs his key to the house then slams the door behind him.

I groan loudly then walk over to the living room. Four year old Lily is coughing up a storm. I give her a sip of water.

Lily grabs my arm and starts crying and screaming silently.

"Daddy went to the market. He should be back soon," I say then held up a spoon of her medicine to her mouth. She frowns and shakes her head and I groan. "Please Lily, please take your medicine for me. I know you don't like it, but the quicker you take it the quicker we get to Storytime," I say. She opens her mouth and takes her medicine. I pick her up and drag her to her room. I tuck her into her bed and pull out her favorite book, *The Tale of The Two Tribes*. "Ready for story time?" I ask her. She nods and looks into my eyes happily.

"The Tale of the Two Tribes. Once there were two great tribes that ruled in our glorious land of Bitotem hundreds of years ago. There was the Tiger Tribe and the Lion Tribe. They were two strong and brave tribes, but they had different views on the world. The Tigers value life in everything and believed that everybody should be equal and in peace. The Lions believed that everyone should follow under one leader and that leader should be King. There was a young boy Lion named Lyell and a young girl Tiger named Tullia. They became friends and later on, fell in love and wanted to get married. The Lion and Tiger Tribes refused to marry them because of their differences. Because of that, Leo and Tyra ran away from the tribes and later had a child together."

I stop reading to look at Lily rubbing her eyes. "Are you sleepy?" I ask her. She shakes her head then yawns. "I know you like this story, but I think we should stop for today and get some rest," I say. She crawls on her hands and knees and bares her teeth like a Tiger and I smile. "I know you like the Tigers, but they are all dead now. Did you hear about the giant fire that killed them all years ago? You probably won't remember Lily, it happened before you were born," I say. She frowns at me then gives me a hug. "I know it's sad. The Tigers seemed like great Bloods. Let's get to bed now and I'll tell you the rest of the story when you wake up ok?" I say.

She nods and lays back in the bed. I pull up the blankets and she rests her head on her soft pillow. I stroke her dirty blonde hair and feel her forehead. *She has another fever again. This is the worst I've seen her. Maybe sleep will help her.* I kiss her cheek and wait until she falls asleep. She closes her eyes, and I stare at my little sister breathing lightly and I slowly stand up from her bed. My eyes get really heavy and I decide to go to sleep.

I am woken up by a loud, echoing cry. I jump out of bed and run swiftly across the hall to Lily's room. Dad is crying, and in his hands little Lily is not moving or breathing. My dad looks at me and his face is red with anger. I silently walk away and go back to my room. I crawl under the covers and stare at the ceiling.

I can still hear the dreadful sobbing of my father in the other room. *This is the first time I've ever seen him cry since mom passed away.* His crying gets softer and softer until the front door slams loudly. I hear the wagon wheels squeak outside and I shift around in my bed. I think of the things that he might do with Lily. Take her to the hospital, go to the cemetery, and bury her next to mom, but I would rather not think about it and sit in silence. I stare only at the darkness around me.

The next morning, I have a raging appetite, which is not normal for me. I go downstairs and have a bigger breakfast than usual. I have two bowls of grapes, three glasses of milk, and five pieces of toast. "Wow, I ate almost the whole fridge!" I walk up to my dad's room to ask him about my appetite. Hopefully he is back from wherever he went last night with Lily. I open his door quietly in case I wake him.

Tiger's Blood

"Dad?" I whisper. No response. I go up and pull the covers from his bed and throw them on the floor. The bed is empty. I start to think that he is still in the hospital with Lily. For a sickly four year old, Lily has been holding strong.

When she was born, the doctor said that she wouldn't live longer than a couple of weeks. She pulled through and was getting a lot better. Lily was a cute sister. She had short, dirty blonde hair, light green eyes, and was a little clumsy. She was my only sibling, but now I know that she is happy in the next life with mom.

I sit on the couch and wait for dad to get home. Ten more hours slowly pass by and there is still no sign of him. This makes me a little mad. I look through the books that we have to see if there is anything about my strange appetite. After skimming through five books, I find no helpful information.

"AAAHH!!" a loud high pitched scream rings in my ears. I hear it again and I run outside to see who is screaming. I see nothing outside and I begin to walk back inside.

"SOMEONE HELP!!!" My ears sting and vibrate to the girl screaming in the distance. *Who is that person screaming?*

I start running in the direction of the screaming voice. I keep walking for 30 minutes or so and I stop when I see her. A little girl who looks five, maybe six. The worst part is she looks like Lily. She is stuck in a steep hole in the ground.

"C-Can you help me?" She asks, sobbing. "Hold on, I'm coming," I say looking around.

I don't have a rope or anything to pull her up with. I feel a strange urge and unexpectedly, I jumped down in the hole. She comes up to me and wraps her arms around my legs. I felt that urge again in my body and my arm twitches. *It's like my body is telling me I have to save her.* I pick up the girl and I place her on my shoulders. She holds on really tightly as I start making my way up the hole.

I slowly go up step by step. I feel my legs wobble but it doesn't stop me. I keep going until I'm on my knees at the top of the hole. The girl climbs off

15

my back and starts walking away. I get up on my feet and brush dirt off my knees.

"Thank you so much," the girl says. I turn to face her, but she is gone. *That was strange.* I look around for a few moments then turn around and go home. *How did I hear a girl screaming from over a mile away? Why did she look like Lily?* I ignore these questions for now and focus on getting back home.
I see my house up ahead of me. There is no wagon in the dirt driveway. He is still not home. This makes me so mad that my hands clench into fists. The least he could've done is left me a note or call me to tell me when he is getting back and where he is. I have a feeling that he left me here on purpose. Does he really hate me so much that he would leave me alone for a day and a half? He has never done anything like this and it makes me worry.

I open the door and the first thing that caught my eye was a note in the middle of the dinner table. That's very odd. That wasn't there this morning, at least I *think* it wasn't there. When I got up this morning, I never saw it. I curiously pick up the note and read it. *Daughter, I am at the hospital with your sister. If you need anything there is food in the fridge. Love you, Father.* At the end of the letter, there is a strange symbol. It was a golden lion symbol with a large, fluffy mane and sharp teeth baring with red blood dripping down the fangs.

There are a couple of things that seem wrong about this letter. The first thing was he called me daughter. He has never called me that before. The second was the symbol. What is that symbol? Is he trying to tell me something? He has never written a symbol on any of his notes before. Come to think of it, he never leaves me notes when he leaves. Questions spin around in my head so fast that it makes me dizzy. I think for a moment before I decide to go to the hospital and see him.

I grab my purple backpack and fill it up with food, water, books, a couple of knives, and the note. I close the door behind me and walk in the direction of the hospital. Because of Lily's medical needs, we needed to live by a hospital. The hospital is about 10 minutes by dads wagon. It shouldn't take me too long to walk there. The ground is dry and hard as I walk at a slow pace. The trees stand tall and they blossom with green leaves and pretty flowers. About 20 minutes later, I arrive at the hospital. I walk in and it is like a dry desert in here. I walk around and see if anyone is here.

"Hello?" I yell. All I hear is my own voice echoing back at me. I walk upstairs and it is as quiet as a ghost. I start getting very curious. He told me he was at the hospital according to the note. This is the only hospital he would go to. *Then why isn't he here?* This makes me so angry. I start pacing around in a circle; my hands turned into fists again. I scrunch up my face and close my eyes tightly while tears race down my cheeks. *I give up, he said he was at the hospital, and I go there and find no one there. He's probably dead now too, what am I going to do?* I start breathing heavy and my heartbeat faster than normal. Before I knew it, I was facing the ground…

I blink my eyes slowly. My body feels heavier than solid gold. I suddenly realize that I am still on the hospital floor. I pick up myself and I notice that I'm walking on all fours. I look down at my feet… they are not feet but paws the size of gloves.

Paws? It sounds creepy when I think of it. I look around for a mirror or something reflective. I try to walk to the bathroom, but I'm not doing do well walking on these paws. I slip and I trip everywhere. I finally stumble my way into a bathroom and look in the mirror and… I see paws, black stripes and white fur, sharp teeth, small round ears, and a…tail? *Well, I'm obviously dreaming.* I close my eyes and try to wake up. I open them and I am still looking at this creature in the mirror. I try to wake myself up. I take one of my claws and pierce it into my other paw. I feel a sharp pain and roar ferociously. I see blood dripping out of my paw then it hit me like a slap to the face. I'm not dreaming. This is real; I never knew that this was who I am. My name is Kira, and I am a Tiger Blood.

2 KIRA

I see a small critter ahead of me, about a couple of yards in front of me. My ears twitch to the sound of its small feet hopping around. I try not to make any movement or sound so I won't scare it off. I slowly crawl then I pounce at my prey. I take one crunchy bite of it's neck and I kill it instantly. The blood of the rabbit drips down my jaws. The flavor of the meat tingles my tongue. I can't eat it now, food is scarce for me. I mutate back into my human form and take my knife out and skin the rabbit.

 I have been out here on my own surviving for four years. I discovered my Tiger Blood when I was 12, and now I'm using it to keep me alive. I almost didn't leave my home, but there were too many reasons for me to go. One, I didn't have any family to go back to. My mother and sister are both dead and my father is missing, I assume he's dead too. Two, the note that my father left me filled me with suspicion. He never left me a note before and when he did, he never came back. Finally, I am set on a new goal, to find the Kingdom of Lions and kill their leader King Andrew. Our world, Bitotem, has been taken over by a strong army of Lion Bloods, well *almost* taken over. The leader of the Lions is Andrew Kingsley, and he has one son I know of named Jett. If I get rid of the son, there will be no bloodline to continue the idiotic rule that is the Kingsley family. They are very well known around the world for the wrong reasons.

The first Kingsley who ruled the Lion's Pride was Alfred Kingsley. He was called the "Skull-crusher King," because of the way he had his enemies killed. He had their head put on a block and he would hammer their heads until the block breaks beneath him. Then there was King "Ralph the Ripper," who would, as you guessed, rip his enemies' limbs off. There was "Hugh the Horror," and "Malcolm the Mad." After Malcolm, King Andrew was born, and he doesn't have a nickname yet. The Kingsleys are determined to kill all of the Bloods who are not Lions, or who are against them. King Andrew is the first king to try and take over all of Bitotem.

Their goal is to be the last Blood standing. So far they have controlled the western side of Bitotem. The funny thing is they think that Lions are the most powerful Bloods in the world. Before the Lions took over, there were about 45 to 50 Tiger Bloods roaming the world. They were so rare that no one would think of another one being alive, until now.

Tiger Bloods are more powerful than Lions. The Lions had known that they couldn't win against the Tiger Bloods, so they did something tragic. They managed to find the only tribe of Tigers, trick them into making peace with them, and ended up killing them.

One night, King Andrew sent a small group of Lions to light their territory on fire. I would imagine that being the most powerful Blood that they would have been able to survive, but even the most powerful Bloods die. What Andrew Kingsley doesn't know was that he didn't kill *all* of the Tigers. Fifteen years later from the fire, and four years from my dad's disappearance, I am the last Tiger Blood standing among this world. The Lions have no idea. *Won't they be surprised?*

Nowadays, I do things on my own. I hunt; I'm good with knives. I use abandoned places for shelter, since most of the Bloods in this world are dead or either living in the Lion's Kingdom. I am heading west. That is where supposedly the Lions are hiding. I've talked to some Bloods along the way about the Lions' territory and almost all of them say the same thing to me, *"You can't see them hiding; they come out of nowhere,"* I believe most of them.

I have heard that their Kingdom is hidden, and I am determined to find out where. Every now and then, I might be sitting in an old shed eating squirrels or rabbits that I've hunted wondering if it's really worth to risk my life for this mission. For someone like me, it's worth everything, so I can make this world right again.

I walk through the deep dark forest and look up to the cloudy sky. The tree's brown leaves begin to float down to the ground. *If the leaves are falling that means that the seasons are changing.* I like the colder season the best. The trees are the nicest in the cold. All their branches are shown and it makes it easier to climb up, hunt the birds, and take their eggs. The most beautiful trees are covered in snow, in my opinion. I feel small drops of rain fall on my face. *I have to find shelter before it starts pouring.*

I come across an old house and slowly open the door. I grip my knife in my hand in case a threat is in there. I look inside and I see nothing, not a speck of life. I immediately walk towards the fridge and see if there is any leftover food. I see soda cans, water bottles, canned foods, and some bread on the counter. Not what I was expecting, but I have to take what I find. I open a can of corn, and I take a slightly bent spoon that I find and eat up. I drink some water, and I sigh loudly. I decide to call it a night and check out upstairs.

I walk into the biggest bedroom and look into the closest for some not ripped clothes. I shuffle around the pile of clothes on the floor and find a plain grey shirt with no sleeves. *No sleeves? Oh well it's clean and that's what matters.* I slip my ripped up, bloody white shirt off and put the grey one on. I find a clean pair of jeans and slip them on. They were a little tight, but still fit great. After that, I curl up into the covers of the bed.

Flashbacks dance in my head with dad and Lily. Lily giggles as dad picks her up and flew her around the room like an airplane. I remember when he used to do that to me. He used to be so happy with us, what happened? *Death tore us apart from each other.* The door suddenly bursts open downstairs interrupting my fantasy.

Heavy panting echoes in my ears. I swiftly get out of bed and take out my pocket knife. I slowly crawl out of the room on my hands and knees and peek down the stairs. A tall, skinny male is looking out the window through the blinds. *Shit... I hope he's not a Lion.* He doesn't seem to notice me, until I move my leg and knock over a small jar. He looks around the room startled.

"Who's there?" He says in a deep voice. He then turns around and looks me straight in the eyes. He has grey eyes like the sky on a rainy day. Chocolate brown hair sits on his scalp. "I see you, come out," he says. I stand up and walk down the steps slowly with the knife in by back pocket. "Who are you?" He asks curiously. I watch his movements closely.

"Kira," I say. He holds out his sweaty hand. "Ethan," he says. I shake his hand then step back. "What were you running from?" I ask. "Umm…Lion Bloods," he says hesitantly. I don't take my eyes off of him. His clothes look very fancy for a normal Blood. He has a dark purple shirt with blue buttons and jeans. Normally purple dye is used for royalty and for wealthy people. He also has black running shoes. "Are you one of them?" I wait for his answer with my right hand on my knife.

Before I know it, I am against the wall with a knife at my throat. He yells, "What are you? A Wolf? Fox? Some kind of Bird??"

I say nothing and take my pocket knife and slash his hand. He steps back and drops his knife. I pick up his knife. He holds his hand tightly and groans in pain. His blood drips down and gets on the carpet. "Why do you want to know what Blood I am?" I ask taking the knife that he dropped, threatening him. He looks back to me then walks in the living room and sits on the couch.

"Forget it, I won't kill you. Do you have anything for this?" he asks holding up his bloody wound. "I don't trust people easily," I tell him. "Oh hey, we have something in common. Now before I change my mind about killing you, can you go get me some gauze or something?" He says sarcastically. I groan disgusted and walk up the stairs to get the gauze from my backpack.

I come back to see him still on the couch. I hand him the gauze and I sit next to him holding my knife. "So are you a Lion or not?" I ask directly. "Yeah I am, but I don't want to kill anyone." He wraps the gauze around his hand. "Then why did you just attack me?" I ask confused.

"I was just trying to scare you, I wasn't actually going to kill you. I wouldn't want to hurt…" he pauses. I look over and see him staring at me.

"…A girl anyway," he finishes. I watch him closely then stand up. "Where are you traveling to?" "The Lions kingdom," I say. He flinches when I say that. "May I ask why?" He asks. "I don't like how your Blood treats other Bloods," I say.

He stares at me for a minute then half smiles. I start walking upstairs and I hear him stand up. "Wait, can I travel with you?" He asks. I look into his cloudy eyes. *He is a Lion, I shouldn't trust him.* "I don't know. I don't normally trust people easily, especially *Lions*," I say. "Can you at least think about it?" He asks me. "Yeah," I say. I walk into the bedroom I was in and get back under the covers. "Goodnight," he says loudly. *It was a good night until you came here.* I bury myself in my soft blanket and fall fast asleep.

"Hey get up," Ethan says shaking my shoulder. "What is it Lion?" I groan. I could hear him growl. "Don't ever call me that again," he hisses at me. "C'mon we have to get out of this area immediately," he shoves my shoulder again. I hop out of bed and grab my backpack. I walk downstairs and peek out the window. Three men covered in armor walk by the house. "Why didn't you tell me that there were more Lions here?" I say angrily. "Because you were sleeping. And they are looking for me, calm down," he says. *Why would Lions be looking for another Lion?*

"We could fight them," I suggest. He nods his head then shuts the blinds. "But what Blood are you? How can you fight?" he asks. *Don't tell him. If he knew then he will probably tell King Andrew.* "I haven't discovered mine yet. I normally just use my knives when I fight," I lie. "Ok, I'll fight them then. You can help me out if I need it," he takes out a knife. *If I even want to help you.* I wanted to say.

I watch him as he hides behind the brown bush in front of the house. The Lions search around and talk to each other. I look back at Ethan and he has his knife in his hand ready to throw. He looks hesitant at first but then he lets it fly. The knife goes into the skull of the blonde haired Lion. The other Lions gasp shockingly as Ethan mutates and pounces on the second Lion. Ethan bares his teeth to the Lion he is attacking, and he claws and bites at his neck. He bleeds out within seconds.

22

My eyes widen when the third Lion mutates and jumps on Ethan. Ethan tries fighting back but this third guy is stronger. He whacks Ethan on the ground with a single hit of his paw. Next thing I notice, I am mutating and stumbling out the door. I run and tackle the Lion on top of Ethan. I claw and bite at his neck with my fangs and I can hear his heart stop beating. I growl intensively and take one final bite to snap his neck. I shake his body around to make sure that he is dead. I crawl off of him and turn around. The blood tastes good against my lips as I lick it off my whiskers. I look up and see Ethan, back in his human form, in awe. I mutate silently and run away from him, fast.

"Kira!!! Kira get back here!!" Ethan screams at the top of his lungs. I keep running, tears forming in my eyes. *Wait… I forgot my backpack.* I stop running when Ethan tackles me ferociously as a Lion. He growls and snarls at me then backs me into a tree. My heart beats loud and fast. *I knew it, he's going to kill me now.* A purple leather bag dangles between his teeth. I groan and take my backpack from him. He mutates and he stomps around angrily. I stand up and try to walk away when he starts talking.

"Kira, why didn't you tell me that you were a fucking Tiger Blood?" He asks. I give him an irritated look. "Why do you think dumbass? I thought you were going to kill me!!" He walks closer to me. "We are enemies, I shouldn't be trusting you with this secret." I say. "I wouldn't tell anyone about this. Just because I'm a Lion doesn't mean I'm unreliable." He says. I sit down on a log and don't say a word.

"I'll just leave then if you don't want me to travel with you." He says. I don't reply. "Fine," he walks away. "Next time I see you around here I *will* kill you," he says angrily. *He hasn't killed me yet, even now that he knows I'm a Tiger Blood.* "You wouldn't kill someone you care for. Even if they *are* your enemies," I say. He turns and looks me straight in the eyes angrily, hesitates for a moment, then vanishes. I get up, brush the leaves off me, and continue to go on my journey alone.

3 ETHAN

I hear the branches snapping under my feet. The leaves rustle as I walk by the trees. I'm on my way back to where dad and Jett are. They have already started to look for me so I might as well go back home. About a month ago, I told them that I was going out "hunting." By hunting, I mean go out and find other Bloods to kill. It's the family tradition, apparently. My dad and brother want me to be a part of this war of Lions versus the world.

Honestly, I want no part of it. It's strange, but my whole family are Lion Bloods all the way back to my great-great grandfather and beyond. I am a Lion Blood as well, but I don't want what most Lion Bloods want. I don't want to own the world and I don't want to kill innocent Bloods. I want to make peace like my mother tried to do years ago. My dad didn't like and agree with her decisions and killed her. He claimed it was an accident and everyone believed him, except me.

I never liked my father's decisions as King. He has always made poor choices. He killed all of the Tiger Bloods left existing when I was young. Well, now I know that's not true. Kira somehow hid that she was a Tiger Blood for four years from the Lions. She is beautiful for a creature, so dangerous and vicious. I wouldn't have even guessed that she was a Tiger Blood. She seems very intelligent. Somehow she sensed that I was a Lion Blood. She looks nothing like how I envisioned a Tiger Blood..

She has messy brown curls that fall to her shoulders, and her dark green eyes look like a beautiful summer meadow. She is short and scrawny, yet she is so aggressive and powerful. I wouldn't want to hurt a special girl like her. My main worry is that another Lion will find her and take her back to my dad as a prize. That shouldn't happen though. Kira is stronger than the Lions, I can feel it.

Tiger's Blood

I look around some more for food to hunt. My stomach growls in anger. It wasn't long until I finally found a dead carcass of a deer that someone left here. I take out my only knife I have left with me and I skin the deer. After my meal, I feel recharged. I get back up and I continue walking north west. My father and brother are a few miles from the edge of Eastern Bitotem. We used to live somewhere else, but I can't really remember it. I was too little, maybe three or four. My dad told me it was destroyed in a fire, then we immediately came here to Eastern Bitotem. After our old home was destroyed, my father built the Lion's Kingdom on Eastern Bitotem…I mean…under it.

Dad wanted to keep the Kingdom hidden so there would not be as many intruders coming into the Kingdom. He had construction workers work on the Kingdom below ground, but it still has the light come in through the skylights. The Kingdom is amazingly built. It has tall brick buildings all compacted together by bridges so people can travel easier. The Kingdom is surrounded by a gigantic wall of bricks with only an entrance door in the front of it. It is so well protected by the wall that there is no need for guards. If I was King, I would still place guards outside the wall just in case of intruders.

There are multiple security cameras built into the wall that cannot be easily seen. There are cameras on every knight that dad sends out too. *Luckily, I damaged the cameras when I attacked those three guards. I know where the cameras are located. I don't want my father to know what I'm doing, especially now there's a Tiger Blood still alive.* Outside the wall, there is a massive river that brings water in and out of the Kingdom. There are two small towers outside the Kingdom with guards to make sure no enemies are coming. Grasslands and dirt cover most of the outside. There are only three secret ways to get in and out of the Kingdom unseen, and one of them leads to my bedroom up in the castle.

There are many buildings and castles throughout the Kingdom. It looks like you are in a whole new world when you live there, it's amazing really. The main town area in the center of the Kingdom is where all the poor Lion Bloods live, including some spared Bloods, which are Bloods other than Lions who my father decided not to kill, but instead, kept as servants. They help work in the Kingdom and they mainly serve the Lion Bloods. They live in these dark, muddy caves on the bottom of the Kingdom.

Tiger's Blood

My best friend Chase lives in the Kingdom with the others; he works in the blacksmith castle. Chase is an Eagle Blood. My father decided not to execute him because he admired Chase's crafty skills, so he kept him as the main blacksmith. I can't wait to get back and see my old friend again. Last time I saw him, he created this new invention. It is a large wooden post with a rope attached to the end of it. My dad liked it so much that he paid Chase 300 gold coins for it. I'm not sure what my dad uses it for, but I just hope it's for good.

 I scavenge around the land looking for a sign of the bush where the hidden entrance is located. I look around and breathe in the air softly. I hear nothing but the sound of my own heart beating in my chest. *It must be around here somewhere. I know I'm close; I can sense it.* I look up into the blue sky and study the thick, fluffy clouds. The clouds collide together and the sky gets gloomy within minutes. *Great, it's going to storm.*

 I look around the forest and search for the biggest tree here. Soon enough, I find a perfect tree and I climb up the trunk. The dark, brown branches leave small cuts and a sticky substance on my hands as I climb up. I finally get to a sturdy branch and wipe my hands clean on my jeans. I rest my head uncomfortably upon a thick and heavy branch and fall asleep quicker than I thought.

The next morning came by quickly. I open my eyes and let out a big yawn. I shake my head and smooth out my thick, brown hair. I stretch my arms and crack my knuckles. I pick a leaf off my shirt and I stand up slowly. I grab onto a branch and balance my body and look below me. The storm last night left only little puddles of mud on the surface. I climb down one branch, then jump and land in a large puddle. The mud splashes on my shirt and jeans and I groan. *Now I really want to find the Kingdom so I can shower and change my clothes.*

I whistle lightly as the branches dance along with the light wind shaking off green and brown leaves. I watch the wind settle down and all the trees fell silent. I close my eyes and take a deep breath of the autumn air. The smell of the nature surrounding me filled me with delight. I decided that today would be a good day to travel.

Tiger's Blood

As I walk through the rainy forest, a strange noise caught my attention. Voices laugh and chuckle in the distance. I look around until I spot five men walking along the trail away from the direction of the Kingdom. "Where would the kid go? He's only seventeen," says the first guy. "I don't know. He said to the King that he was going out hunting, but he's been gone for quite some time," says the dark haired male who is shorter than the first man. I quickly climb back up the tree I slept in and watch the men walk below me.

"Well he's the King's son guys, and that's why we have to find him. If we don't bring Ethan back to King Andrew soon then we are all next in line to be hanged," The larger one remarks. I recognized the symbol on their armor, and they're knights of the Lions guard. Two of the guards have crossbows in their arms while the other three have swords. Snapping and cracking fill my ears as I notice the branch I was on was slowly breaking. Without warning, the branch snaps off and I fall hard on the ground. I groan in pain as I quickly stand up. The Lions turn around and look me in the eye. "Hey, that's him! It's Prince Ethan guys get him!" One of the guys yells.

I quickly take my knife and throw it in the neck of the first guy. His body flops to the ground as the others spring toward me. I mutate and barrel straight at them. They move out of my way as I run the opposite direction I was heading in. I hear them yell and scream as one of them starts shooting arrows at me. One hit me in the paw, but I just shook it off. My dark brown mane flows around as their voices become distant. I slow my pace when I realize that they stopped chasing me. *Great they are going back to the Kingdom to tell my dad that they spotted me. Now he's going to send even more guards out.* I watch as I mutate and my paws became hands and feet and my claws became fingernails. I rub my palm as a small trickle of blood ran down my hand. I look at my bandaged hand and I instantly think of Kira. *After they tell my father they saw me, they will double the guards at night. They might find Kira; surely, she is still around here.* I look back once more to make sure they stopped following me and I sigh loudly. I then start running back towards Kira to warn her about the Lions that will soon be coming.

4 KIRA

The bushes rattle loudly as I open my eyes instantly from my dreams. Deep growling fills my ears with suspicion. I pull a dull knife out and grip it firmly in my hand. A dark shadow slowly walks out of the bush in front of me. Glowing yellow eyes stare at my motionless body. The grey Wolf Blood bares his sharp teeth at me. He slowly steps closer to me until we are face to face. I show him my knife and scrape it lightly against his muzzle just enough so it would scare him. "Just one more move and I'll kill you," I warn him. He backs up and mutates into a tall, tan teenager. His dark brown eyes look at me bravely. "Ugh finally. I've been looking for you everywhere!" He exclaims. I look at him puzzled. "Excuse me?" I say, confused.

"You're that *special* girl who killed the Lions the other day," he smiles and raises his eyebrows. *He saw me fighting…he knows…* "How do you know that?" I ask curiously. "I was hunting and when I saw those Lions I hid. I was waiting for them to walk by, then you came out and ripped through them like they were nothing," the tall black haired boy says. I study him closely. "Are you going to kill me?" I grip my knife again. "A *White* Tiger Blood? Why would I kill such a beautiful creature like yourself? Especially since you are the last one left," he chuckles and smiles brightly. I look around nervously in case someone overheard. He holds his hand out to me. "I'm Noah." I politely give him a firm handshake. "Kira," I say. "That's a pretty name," he says. He rubs my hand with his thumb and I yank my hand away.

I pick up my backpack and start walking away. "Where you going? We just met," he asks desperately. "Away from here," I say. He chuckles then grabs my shoulder. "Can I go with you princess?" He asks. "You don't even know where I'm going or who I am and you want to follow me?" I laugh. He scratches his head. "Yeah well, I don't have anywhere else to go.

Tiger's Blood

I don't have a certain place I'm going; I just wander around Bitotem and hunt and sleep. I'm a 'Lone Wolf' you might say," he laughs. I look him straight in the eyes.

He's no threat, I can tell, but he also knows that I'm a Tiger. If I say no he could go tell somebody about my existence. It would be better to keep him close by so I can make sure my secret stays a secret. I sigh loudly and nod my head. "Fine let's go, but I'm not a princess," I groan. "Well you are pretty like one," Noah smiles and follows behind me. I roll my eyes, ignore that comment, and keep walking.

I don't even know if I can trust him. Well, to be honest I trust him more than Ethan right now. Ethan threatened to kill me if he sees me again. I know he won't kill me. He hesitated before he said that he would. I can read through people's actions and emotions and facial expressions. It's not that hard to figure out. Just like how I can tell that Noah was trying to flirt with me. I'm not into flirting or dating. I feel like it distracts me from my goals in life, especially now. I hope he figures that out before I have to tell him directly.

We keep on walking for a few more hours until we reach a lake. The dark pool of water glistens in the moonlight ahead of us. The lake stretches out in a large crooked oval with ridges and curves. A lonely island sits in the middle of the lake with a single tree. Noah turns his head to look at me and I sit down against the grass. "We can stop here for the night," I say as I take a blanket out.

Noah crouches down next to me and stretches on the ground. I curl up in my blanket and close my heavy eyes. Morning comes to me quickly. I stretch my arms and rub the sleep from my eyes. Down by the water Noah is mutated trying to fish, but he isn't doing very well. I clean up my mess and I sling my backpack around my shoulder. "C'mon Noah we have to leave." I say. He mutates back and follows me.

Six days of traveling and I feel worn down now that I have a companion. He always needs to stop to do something from bathroom stops to hunting. This will definitely make my trip feel endless. I don't know where we are, I don't know when we will get to the Lions Kingdom or where Ethan is going. All I know is I'm tired from walking. We finally come to a stop next to a beautiful 30 foot waterfall that splashes down on slick, mossy rocks below.

I put my purple bag down and take some squirrel carcasses out. I rip into the flesh with my knife as Noah stares in awe at the waterfall. Since we are running low on food I'm only eating once every few days. I can go up to four days without food; unfortunately, Noah eats everything I catch. I chow down on the tender meat when I get splashed with water.

"Hahahahaha," Noah chuckles. "Sorry hun, I'm just trying to catch a fish," he says. I frown, irritated. The seventeen year old stands in the crystal clear water shirtless and motionless. His eyes focus on a moving object in the water. "What are you looking at?" I say. He holds up his pointer finger to his mouth then his hands disappear under the water. I watch his movements as he swiftly dove under the water and was wrestling with something bigger than a normal fish. A minute later he proudly holds up a large sized fish to me. "Nice catch," I act impressed. "Let's cook him up!" He says and crawls out of the water.

I start the fire and let Noah cook the fish. I take a couple small bites of the fish and let Noah have the rest. Noah dries his shirt next to the fire and he puts it back on. I walk towards the small lake next to the waterfall and roll the tip of my finger across the water. The ripples flow smoothly through the lake. I feel comfort come to me through watching the water lightly bounce up and down. I sit there and bury my head in my thoughts.

What would happen if to me if the Lions defeated me? They probably wouldn't care. They'd celebrate my death. Maybe even make it a holiday and have a gathering every year and have a large feast in honor of my death. All except Ethan. Ethan wouldn't celebrate. He would be upset or maybe feel the one responsible for my death. When I met him he didn't seem like the kind of person who would want anyone killed, well after he tried to kill me. He did resist killing me, even after he found out my Blood. I respect him for that.

We soon leave the scenery and get back on our feet. I look around the forest to see if there was anyone following us. "Do you think we are getting close?" Noah asks. "I don't know. Maybe, we have been walking for a while," I say. He nods then smiles. "I have a question for you, if I may." I look at him curiously and nod. "Why is such a pretty and tough girl like yourself willing to fight the Lions and possibly get killed?" He asks.

"I want peace in this world. I want what every Blood wants, equality. Well, every Blood except the Lions. I don't want anyone to treat me differently because I may possibly be the last Tiger Blood left in Bitotem. We are all Bloods no matter what. I hate that Andrew and his son want to kill innocent Bloods for the sake of them not being Lion's or for disagreeing with them. It just makes me sick thinking about it," I say. "Alright I was wrong. You are pretty, tough, and good-hearted," Noah smiles with his perfect teeth. His smile gives me a feeling of joy. A loud shriek interrupts our talking. Someone else is near.

5 ETHAN

I push the leaves and branches out of my way as I walk forward. The brown leaves crunch beneath my feet as I stomp on the ground. *I must be close, Kira shouldn't have gone too far in this part of the woods.* "Ugh Noah keep up with me, please." I hear a familiar voice not too far. "Kira?" I yell hoping for a response. I look through the trees and see a small figure. "Ethan?" She replies. I see her body hidden in the trees and I smile. *Thank goodness she's alive.*

I walk her way and I stop when I see her face staring angrily at me. "What are you doing here?" She sneers. "I came back to warn you about more Lions coming," I say truthfully. She crosses her arms in front of her chest. "Why did you *really* come back?" She scowls. "I came back because I worry about you. You are a Tiger, anybody out here could kill you or take advantage of you," I confess.

"That's funny, cuz I could have sworn that last time we talked you said that you would kill me next time you see me in the woods," she smirks. I open my mouth to say something when a tall, tan stranger with thick black hair walks out of the bushes and stands next to Kira. I close my mouth and watch him closely. "Hey Kira look what I found," he says holding out small red and blue berries in his hand. "Put them back, they are probably poisonous. I'll do all the hunting and scavenging," she says not taking her eyes off of me. "Who is this?" The mysterious male looks at me curiously.

"This is Ethan; he's a Lion Blood," Kira says calmly. The dark haired teen grabs Kira's arm and takes a few steps back. Kira rolls her eyes. "Noah, if he was going to kill us then he would have done it already," Kira says sarcastically. Noah steps forward again hesitantly. I nod and I glance at Kira. "Could I speak to you alone Kira? Please?" I beg her. She eyes me carefully then glances over at Noah. He looks back at her nervously. "Will he hurt you?" I hear Noah whisper. "No he won't, it's safe. Go build us a fire while I talk to Ethan," she commands. He nods then disappears in the woods.

Kira sits down on a muddy log and looks up at me with her greenish-grey eyes. "Tell me everything. Why did you come back?" She asks again. *I thought I told her twice already. Maybe she just doesn't believe me.* I sit down on the muddy log next to her. "I was walking along a trail when I saw five Lion Blood guards walking towards me and I climbed up a tree. I fell out of the tree and they saw me and tried to kill me, but I ran away from them. They chased me for a little while but they gave up and left. I then heard your voice, so I followed it. I honestly did come back because I wanted to warn you, but also because I thought that they would find you before I did and find out your Blood," I say. She nods then stands up. "Ok, I believe you. Are the Lions that chased you close?" she asks.

"I don't think so," I say and stand up next to her. "Ok, let's go eat I'm starving," she says then walks over towards the fire. I sit down close to the burning orange flames and look around the area. Kira's purple backpack sits next to me while Kira cooks up a part of a fish. I notice a slip of paper fall out of the side pocket of the bag and I pick it up. I walk over to Kira and nudge her shoulder. "This fell out of your backpack," I say and hand it to her. "Thanks," she opens it up slowly. When she opens it, I notice that it is a letter with a symbol at the end of it. I examine the symbol closely and stand back appalled. *I know that symbol.* Kira turns around to me. "What is it?" she asks.

"That symbol on the letter, that's the symbol of the Lion Bloods," I explain to her. She looks at me confused then examines the letter over. "I got this letter four years ago after my father disappeared *and* right before I discovered my Tiger's Blood," she says. "I don't know why it's on there; all I know is that is the symbol for Lions," I say. She grumbles frustrated then puts the letter back in her backpack.

Kira looks up to the darkening sky and sighs. She takes a blanket out of her backpack and curls up on the short, green grass and closes her eyes. I feel myself smile when I look at her sleep. I glance over at Noah and he looks back at me. He gives me half a smile then looks at the ground. *He still fears me.*

I walk over to Kira and lay down next to her. She breathes softly as she sleeps. I gulp nervously hoping not to wake her up. I think about the Lion symbol on her letter. *What was that? Did my father send that letter four years ago? If he did why? He doesn't use the Lion's symbol unless it's for something important.*

I sit in silence and watch her sleep silently. Noah fell asleep about an hour ago. Most of the time I don't sleep; I just can't fall asleep sometimes. The sun starts coming up and the fire is barely lit anymore. I get some more sticks and wood and throw them in the weak fire. *I hate that I'm a Lion.* The Lions are cruel animals. Once they find out about that Kira is a Tiger Blood, they'll find a way to kill her. I should be the one to protect her, but she is heading straight towards the danger.

I don't know if I should tell her to turn around or to lead her towards the Lion's Kingdom. Maybe I could do something else. I know exactly where my dad and brother are. Kira still doesn't know that I am King Andrews's youngest son. *Well how would she know? My father doesn't really talk about me much in Kingdom or in general. He hates me.* She might freak out if she finds out or not trust me anymore. *If she even trusts me now.*

Maybe I could lead her and Noah in the wrong direction. I could lead them, but then I would have to leave them. I have to go back to the Kingdom and go to my dad and show him that I am ok. He wouldn't send so many Lion's if he didn't want me back. *Would he even care if I'm ok? He has always hated me my whole life. I am curious about that note that Kira has. I want to ask my father about that.* I must get back to my family somehow before the reward for me gets higher. It's going to take a while to figure out, but this plan just might work.

"Hey Kira get up," I say lightly shaking her shoulder. She yawns then stretches out her arms. She stands up then looks at me. She then walks over and taps Noah on the head. "Get up loser we are traveling early today," she says humorously. Noah then stands up and walks slowly to Kira. She bumps my arm and starts walking with Noah following behind her. "Wait Kira, I know where we should go," I say. She turns around to face me. I point behind me. "The Lions chased me that way, so I think we are close to the Kingdom," I tell her. "Fine, you lead the way then," Kira says, irritated.

Tiger's Blood

My father will kill me if he finds out that I'm traveling with a Tiger Blood. He expects me to kill Bloods that are not Lions, especially Tigers. He hates Tiger Bloods. I don't know why he had to kill off the Tiger population, but I don't see anything bad about them. Kira could actually benefit the kingdom. She could show the Kingdom that Tigers are good Bloods and that my father was wrong to kill them. I can't take her back now though, there are too many guards searching for me. I can't risk them finding Kira. I have to go back home and show him that I'm ok and alive.

We walk for what seems like hours and we come to a place to rest. I glance over at Noah and I see him flirt with Kira a little bit. I hardly know Noah, and he is already annoying me. Kira should be smart enough not to flirt back with him or give him the attention he wants from her. I don't think she feels the same way as he does. She doesn't seem like the person who likes to date. I don't know though, girl's feelings can be confusing, *very* confusing. I never got along with the girls back at the Kingdom.

The only things the girls saw in me was my royalty. All the Lion girls back at the Kingdom wanted to be a princess. I don't understand the big deal with being a princess. I hate being a prince already, and I don't want to marry a girl just because she wants to be a princess. I don't want someone to date or marry me because I am a prince either. I especially don't want to marry another Lion unless they are like me and hate other Lions. My thoughts disappear as I continue walking with the beautiful girl alongside me.

6 NOAH

We have been traveling for about a month now. I don't know where we are, but I do know that Kira has been acting very strangely lately. She has been fainting multiple times a day. She has been walking very slowly, and she won't eat as much as she used too. I am worried sick about her ever since she started these random dizzy spells. I blame it on the late season heat. The warmer season is about to finish, then the cold season will come. Even I, as a Wolf Blood get overheated in the hot seasons. My pelt feels hot and sticky and I sometimes pass out randomly. I offered to let Kira ride on me if she is tired but she keeps denying it.

We walk around the deep, green woods a little longer until I spot a long, grey path. I stop and run over towards the path. "Hey Kira look at this," I call to her. She soon stands by my side looking at the broken, grey path. "What's so exciting about this?" she asks me. I point over to the large sign next to the path and she squints her eyes. The sign reads, "Beware, stay out of the Lion's Kingdom if you wish to live," with scratched out letters. I smile at her and she smiles back.

"The Lions territory is really close to here. We are only a couple miles away," I explain to her. "Oh yeah, that is true. Good job Noah," she says and pats me on the back. I look up at the grey skies and frown. The fluffy clouds begin to form together in a giant cloud. "It looks like it's going to storm though," I say. "We should find a shelter then," Kira says. I look over at Ethan and he has his hands in his pockets staring off into space. I can feel the negative pressure in the air whenever I'm around him.

I have a feeling that Ethan doesn't trust me. I don't know why, because I'm not a bad guy. At least I think I'm a good person. Unless you ask my family. I was the oldest of five siblings. I had two brothers and two sisters. My brothers were Kai and Scout and my sisters were Iris and Avery. My brothers hated me because I was the oldest and I got everything. That wasn't true though. My parents loved all five of us, but they despised me the most. They never told me why they hated me, but they just did. I felt like I was alone and no one knew how I felt.

When I discovered my Wolf Blood at sixteen, they made me do all the hunting and gathering food for them. My mom was a Fox Blood and my father was a Falcon. I believe they were disappointed that I wasn't a Fox or a Falcon like them. Two of my siblings were Falcons and the other two were Foxes. I ended up getting fed up with all the shit they made me do and I ran away. I don't even know if they are still alive or not, then I found Kira and I couldn't be happier. Well, if she likes me back, I'll be even happier.

We travel along the grey path until we came to a dead end. I find a cave that would be a good enough shelter until the storm dies down. Ethan helps me start a fire and I take some of the fish that is left to eat. After we lit the fire, we notice that Kira hasn't come in the cave yet. Ethan walks to the end of the cave and I follow him. We watch as Kira stands in the rain with her arms straight to her sides. She starts dancing and running around in the rain. She twirls and laughs as her beautiful brown hair gets drenched. She falls down in a mud puddle then stands up and walks over to the cave, all dirty and sticky.

"What was all that about?" I ask her curiously. "I used to dance in the rain all the time when I was little. I love how the rain feels. My parents would get mad at me because I would always get dirty," she giggles. I smile at her and so does Ethan. "Well, you are a beautiful dancer," Ethan adds. I nod in agreement and sit down by the fire. Kira scrapes off the sticky mud from her clothes and hair. Ethan sits at the entrance to the cave looking out at the rain falling. He lets out a big sigh then crawls over to Kira.

I watch as Ethan and Kira giggle and whisper to each other. I could feel a pinch of hurt inside of me and I just lay down and pretend to sleep as I listen to their conversation. "You know I can make you a sword if you want," Ethan says. "Really? How?" Kira asks. "I have a friend who makes really good swords. I could have him make you one," He explains. "What friend?" she asks. "He lives in the Lion Kingdom," he says.

"Why did you leave the Lion's Kingdom?" she asks. "We were running low on food, so I went out hunting when I got lost and I couldn't find my way back. When we find our way back, I could find my friend and look for a sword for you," he says. "That would be really nice if I had a larger weapon with me. My pocket knife can't do as much as I want it to; therefore, I would prefer a one handed sword so I could kill my enemies quicker," she laughs. "I'll keep that in mind," Ethan says and then they were silent.

The sun shines brightly in my face and wakes me up. I yawn and stretch my arms out. I look over and Kira squirms around in her sleep. After that I noticed something: Ethan's missing. I get up quietly and look outside the cave. He is nowhere to be found: *I knew that Lion was trouble. He is off to go tell the others about Kira.* I sit back down and I stare at Kira slowly waking up. She stretches her arms out then rubs her eyes. She looks to the back of the cave then back at me. She gets up and looks around her area and storms angrily to the end of the cave. She walks outside then runs back in the cave.

"Noah, you didn't even notice that Ethan was gone?" she says in an angry tone. "I just woke up and noticed," I reply. She looks through her backpack frustrated. "He took the note with him," she grumbles angrily. She packs up everything and storms out of the cave. "Hey, maybe this is a good thing. He probably left because he was mad or upset. Now it can just be the two of us again together," I say and smile. She turns around and lightly punches me in the gut. I groan in pain.

"Noah are you insane? We need him on this journey," she says frustrated. I start following behind her. "Are you sure that we need him? Or is it that *you* need him?" I ask her. She stops walking then turns to face me. "Listen, we are going to find him whether you like it or not. Now let's go," she says angrily then keep on walking. *I guess that answered my question.* I frown and I follow Kira's footsteps.

7 ETHAN

I tried forcing myself to stay, but I just couldn't. I have to go back to my dad to let him know that I'm ok. *If he even cares that I'm ok.* I want to ask about this note that Kira got four years ago. I fold up Kira's note and put it in my pocket. Even though my plan was to leave, I didn't want to leave. I just feel like I have to right now. I'll be back for Kira, and I'll even get her that sword that she wants. If only I could sneak in and grab her a good sword or ask Chase to make one for me. It shouldn't take him more than a few days to make a sword for Kira. I look around to see if anyone is close before pushing a large bush out of my way. *I forgot dad uses artificial bushes instead of real bushes for the hidden entrances.* I examine the hole under the bush and slowly crawl down inside it. I land in what used to be my old bedroom and I cover up the hole.

My dad uses holes like the one I just crawled in through to trap Bloods and kill them. He either lures Bloods in or just goes out and kidnaps them without warning. I disagreed with that and my dad just ignored me. It's really hard when you try and speak out but nobody will listen to you. That has been basically my whole life, which is why I ran away and why I don't give out my opinion anymore.

I stand up and brush the dirt off my jeans. I walk out of my room and everyone stares at me. They suddenly get on their knees and bow to me. Royalty has its strange perks to it I guess. I've never liked being a prince though, everyone expects things from you and all I've done is talk back to my father. If I become King one day, I'm going to stop the war and make peace like the world was again. I won't be King for at least thirty years though, maybe more if my brother decides to have kids. That's what sucks about being the younger brother in a royal family; I won't be King unless both my brother and father die and if Jett doesn't have kids. My brother is next in line, like he's going to do any good to this Kingdom.

A guard spots me and quickly runs over to me. *Shit, now I'm in trouble.* "Prince Ethan, King Andrew has been searching for you. You must go see him at once," the tall guard says to me. "Thank you, I'll definitely consider this offer," I say and try to walk away from him. The guard then grabs me by the arm aggressively and chuckles as he leads me towards the throne room. "That wasn't an offer Prince Ethan; the King needs to see you now," he says. When we get there he lets go of my arm, and I walk in and see my dad sitting there with his shiny golden crown atop his head.

"Ethan," his deep voice calls my name. I walk up to my dad and look him straight in his dark, careless eyes. "Where have you been the past two months, son?" he asks. "Oh you know…just killing Bloods and hunting…and stuff," I lie through my teeth. He laughs deeply then catches his breath. "Don't lie to me boy. I know where you have been. Have you forgotten about our security cameras?" he asks me. "No I haven't," I say. "That I know is true because I see you have been destroying over half of our finest tree cameras," he says then shows me a video on the camera screen behind him.

The video shows me traveling with Kira and Noah. I look directly into the camera and smash it with a stick then the camera feed shuts off. I swallow nervously then look back at my father. "Who are those Bloods you are traveling with?" He asks me with a smug look on his face. "Well, the male is a Wolf Blood. I'm not sure what the girl is," I lie again. He squints at me then frowns. "Hmm ok," he grumbles. *He doesn't know that Kira is a Tiger, that's good.* I turn around and try to leave the room, but two guards block the exit. "Wait son, I have a mission for you," he says sharply.

I turn around and look up at him. "If you do not complete this mission entirely then you are not allowed back here again. Do you understand son?" he asks. I nod my head and he continues. "You are going to go back out there and kill those two Bloods that you have been traveling with. If you fail this, then I'd might as well just throw you in jail with the rest of those traitors. Prove to me that you are truly my son, and you will get more respect from me and the rest of the Kingdom," he says sharply. *I'll take those chances. Even if I do kill Kira and Noah, he still won't have any respect for me.* I swallow deeply then nod. "Good, now you should be on your way-"

"Wait," I interrupt him. He looks at me puzzled. "What?" he asks irritated. "I need more weapons, perhaps a sword?" I asks him. "Very well son. Jett!!" He cries out. My older brother walks in the room dressed in all black. His hair is spiked up a little with pale skin like mine, and he has a smirk on his face. "Yes father?" he asks. "Take your brother to Chase and see that he gets a new weapon," he says. Jett nods and he gives me an evil glare. We leave the throne room and he takes me downstairs to the blacksmith room. He shoves me and growls deeply at me. *What's his problem?* I walk into the blacksmiths room and I look at all the wonderfully designed weapons around me. There were bows, swords, knives, crossbows, shields, you name it. A large crashing sound catches my attention and I turn to see my old friend, Chase.

Chase and I grew up together. He has dirty blonde hair with blue eyes and light skin. He is as tall as me and has always been a loyal friend to me. When we were little we used to play with each other all the time. We loved to role play together; I would be the bad guy and he would be the one defeating me. He would make us stick swords and shields made of logs and leaves and we would pretend to fight each other. We would swim in the river when it got hot outside and play with cards. We had a lot of fun together when we were little. He started making and designing weapons when he was nine out of scraps of metal and wood. Now he is the head weapon maker for the Lions, even though he's not a Lion. He is a very skilled Eagle Blood.

"Why hello most noble and handsome Prince Ethan, I haven't seen you in a while," he jokes around. We both laugh and I walk over and give him a hug. "How have you been Chase?" I ask. He frowns. "Well, I do wish that the Lions would give me a raise, but otherwise I have been living here happily," Chase says. "Well, I can talk to my dad about a promotion for you," I say. He smiles.

"You've always had a good heart Ethan. I wish you were the King here. You would be an excellent King," he says. I smile at him. "No I wouldn't be a good King. It's a nice thought though," I laugh. Chase smiles and rubs his hands together. "Now what sort of weapon would you like?" he asks politely. I lean in close to him. "I actually need you to make me a special sword," I whisper. "It must be so special because you have to whisper it to me," Chase whispers back jokingly.

I explain the detail and the design for the sword I want him to make for Kira. I remember the cool design that she explained to me in the cave about the purple swirls and the leather handle for the sword she wants. "It has to be a one handed sword and make it unique. This isn't going to be for just *any* random Blood," I say. "Easy, that shouldn't take me longer than a couple hours since I was already in the process of making a one handed sword," he smiles. He begins to create the sword and I look around at some of the tools and materials that Chase has. "Hey, do you think I could use some of these?" I ask Chase. "Use whatever you need buddy," he says and I nod in response.

I take some leather, metal, and some screws. I make two brown leather straps and I wrap it together to make a nice cover for my knife. After I make that, I take some old rusted metal, and bend it into a circular handle. I then take one of Chase's metal blades and attach it to the handle. I hold up the knife and grip it to make sure that it stuck together. The blade came apart, so I pick up a new blade and make it tighter. I lightly touch my pointer finger to the tip of the blade and I chuckle to myself. "Awesome,"
I whisper to myself. I hide the blade in my pocket and wait for Chase to be done.

"Here you go Ethan," Chase says holding out a beautiful silver sword with the swirl design in purple and a leather handle. I stand there breathless and he hands me the sword. *It's a little heavier than I wanted it to be, but that's alright.* "This looks amazing Chase, you really are talented," I compliment him. "Hey, it's my job. I've been doing this for nine years. I know how to deliver," he laughs. He hands me the case for the sword and I thank him. "She's going to love this sword," I whispered to myself. "She? Is our beloved Prince Ethan finally taken interest in women?" Chase laughs. "Haha, no not in women. In a certain *woman.* She's a special girl who deserves a one of a kind sword," I say.

"Well, I hope this special girl likes this custom made sword," Chase says. "I know she will," I say. I pat him on the back then I leave the room. Just as I was about to leave, my dad comes up to me. He grabs my shoulder. "Remember son, I want those kids dead. I don't want one of my Lions coming back here telling me that my son is hanging around two other Bloods," he says. I deeply swallow and nod. "Yes sir," I say. He lets go of my shoulder and I walk up to my room.

I walk inside my room and close the big wooden door. I sit on my bed with my dark blue blanket and I stare at the pictures on the wall. I take off the portrait of my family and put it in my lap. My father frowns in the picture as usual. My brother sits proudly in my father's lap. The baby version of me sits in my mother's arms and smiles happily with only three teeth in my mouth. My mother looks at me and smiles with the prettiest smile. She had curly brown hair and grey eyes like mine. *I miss you mom. Even if I didn't know you for long, I still miss you.* I put the portrait back on the wall and climb out of the hole in my room. I cover the hole up with the bush and start walking.

I put Kira's sword in the case and sling it around my shoulder. I walk around in the dark night and follow my tracks where I came from. I hope that Kira is alright. She'll love the sword that I made just for her. The problem is she is going to ask where I got the materials to make a sword. I don't know whether to lie to her or tell her the truth. *I should be honest with her. She might be angry that I went back to the Kingdom without her. Maybe I shouldn't tell her.* I look around me for a spot to rest and I stop for the night. I struggle to climb up into the closest tree and lie down on a slick branch. I close my eyes and listen to the crickets sing their songs in the dark night.

8 KIRA

"Ethan!!! Ethan!!" I scream loudly to the sky hoping for a response. "Kira give it up we have been searching for three weeks!" Noah says irritated. I turn and growl deeply at him. *Why does he have to be so selfish?* I'm really starting to get annoyed with him. I thought I sort of liked him, but now he's just been complaining lately. "Ethan!" I scream one more time. No response. "Kira, can we rest please?" Noah groans. "Ugh fine, let's stop here," I say. We stop in the middle of the forest and Noah sits down and falls asleep almost instantly.

How are we supposed to find Ethan in the forest when the whole world of Bitotem is made up of forests and lakes? It took me four years to get even somewhat close to the Lion's Kingdom. Now I meet a Lion who knows the way to the Kingdom and he betrays me and runs off. That stupid traitor. He probably went back to tell someone that he found a Tiger Blood. Maybe they'll cut my head off and place it in a shiny case as a prize. I try to fall asleep hoping that we will find Ethan soon.

A loud crack of a branch woke me up immediately. I look over to Noah and shake his shoulder. "Noah get up I hear something," I say. He groans angrily then stands up. "I don't hear any-" he stops and stares up at something above me. "Kira..." he starts to say. I stand motionless. "What?" I ask. In a quick moment he stands up, grabs my waist and pulls me down on the ground as I hear a loud crash behind me. "Noah!" I yell angrily before realizing that a tree branch almost fell on me. "Oh...thank you," I say and he smiles. "No problem little Tiger," he winks at me. A second later, a person crashes down from the tree.

I grab my knife and Noah grabs me and pulls me away. "Let go of me!" I protest. "I'm sorry, but I'd rather not get hit by falling things today. I don't want you hurt," he says. I scoff and the person grumbles and stands up. I catch a quick glance of a weapon around his waist and I arm my knife again.

44

He brushes his fingers through his scalp and eyes me. "Kira!" He says excitedly. *Ethan?* He brushes off some dirt and leaves and waddles over to me. "What were you doing in the tree?" I question him.

"Trying to get some sleep," he says then smirks. "Guess someone woke up on the wrong side of the branch," Noah laughs. I glare over at him angrily and he stops laughing. Ethan walks towards me then grabs his leg in pain. "You ok" I ask. He shakes his head and I examine his left leg. "You just have some bad bruising. It'll heal up soon," I assure him. He nods at me. "I wouldn't sleep in trees anymore though," I smile at him. "Obviously," He rolls his eyes and smiles back. I notice that he still has that gash in his hand from where I cut him when we met. "Hey I'm sorry for cutting you," I say looking at the scar. "It's okay, you were just trying to defend yourself," he smiles. I smile back and we keep walking.

We walk for about an hour when Noah stops again. "Please Kira, can we take a break?" He says then lies down in the dirt. "We just stopped not too long ago Noah," I say. Ethan sits down with him and I groan. "Fine," I say and press my body up against a tree. I move around to get comfortable, when I glare at Ethan and look down at his hip. *What is that weapon he has?* "Ethan?" He looks over to me. "Yes?" he says. I point down at his waist. "What's that on your waist?" I ask. "Well I was going to give it to you later, but I guess now is a good time," he says. He stands up and unsheathes the weapon. The sword glitters in the sunlight. "Whoa…" I stand up breathless. "And this is for me?" I ask him.

"Yup, here try it out," he says and hands it to me. My arms tremble at the weight of it, but that doesn't stop me. *It will feel lighter the more I use it.* I walk up to a small tree and swing the sword violently, breaking the branches as I go. The leaves fly around me as I grunt and strike the defenseless tree. *It has a sharp bite, but is it sharp enough for me?* Within seconds, the tree falls down in front of me. "I think she's got the hang of it," Noah chuckles. Ethan laughs along with him then I look to both of them. As I walk back to them, the sword slips in my hands and it cuts me deeply on my left arm.

I wince in pain as my blood drips down my arm and trickles down the silver sword. "Are you ok??" Ethan says and runs towards me. Noah came over and helps me stand up. I chuckle and I pick the sword up and hold it in front of my face. I watch as the blood shed and ripple down the sword, splitting my reflection in half. "Yes I'm ok," I reply to Ethan. "It hurt you pretty bad huh?" Noah remarks. "*She* hurt me really bad," I correct him. "She? Who's she?" Ethan asks. "*Bloodshed*, my sword," I explain. "Hah, that's a cute name," Noah laughed. I groan. "It's not supposed to be cute Noah, it's supposed to be intimidating," I snap. "Ah, intimidating just like you," Noah laughs. I glare at him angrily and he stops laughing. "I like the name, it suits you. Do you like the sword?" Ethan asks.

"I love it," I say and smile wide at him. Ethan hands me the case. "Here she's all yours now," he says and winks. I put *Bloodshed* in her case and look up to Ethan. *How did he randomly come across a weapon like this in the forest?* "Where did you get this?" I ask him curiously. He struggles to get the words out of his mouth. "I um killed a Lion Guard who was chasing me and I took it from him," he stutters then gives me a nervous smile. I look him in the eyes. "Hmm, ok," I say and I walk past him and scowl. *He just lied to me. I can tell by the way he stutters.*

After walking for a few hours, we all start getting tired and stop for the night. I put my backpack down and take out my blanket, when one of my books fall out of the backpack. I pick it up and read the title. *The Tale of The Two Tribes.* I smile and open up the first page. I read the story and think to myself about the Lion Tribe and the Tiger Tribe. *This was Lily's favorite book. She loved how Tullia and Lyall fell in love and had a child together. She loved girly things like that. Although she was only five when she passed and didn't know much about the world. She was so sweet and innocent. She didn't know anything about how the real world is like and how crazy the Bloods are here. I'm glad she passed away early, so she wouldn't have to live in this messed up world.*

"Are you ok Kira?" Noah whispers to me. I look up from my book and stare into Noah's brown eyes. "What?" I say. "Kira you're crying, are you ok?" he asks. "Oh, yeah, yeah I'm ok," I say wiping away my tears. *I didn't even realize that I was crying.* "I was just reading this old book that I used to read to my little sister back home," I say showing him the book. "*The Tale of The Two Tribes?* I've never heard of that story before, but that's sweet that you would tell your sister that story. How old is she?" he asks.

"She was five. She passed away the day before I discovered my Blood," I say. *Lily would have loved seeing my Tigers Blood. If only she lived a day longer.* "I'm so sorry. Can I help you in any way?" Noah asks. "No. You probably don't know how it feels to lose someone close to you," I say. "Actually I do know. I left my family willingly. I don't know if any of my siblings or my parents are alive or dead right now. That scares me and makes me feel sad," Noah says. "I'm sorry, that is sad," I say. He nods.

"Hey Noah, I have a question," I say. "Sure, what is it?" he responds. "How did you discover your Wolf Blood?" I ask. He smiles at me. "It's an interesting story. I was hunting with my two little brothers, Kai and Scout, one day because we were running low on food. While we were walking, I noticed that I had a stronger sense of smell and I could hear things from miles away. I turned around and Scout was missing. I listened for him and I heard him scream. Kai and I ran until we found him with two Lion guards. Kai ran away to get our parents. The Lions were about to get me when I suddenly mutated for the first time as a Wolf. I felt threatened and I attacked the two guards. We fought until they bled out and died. Scout was covered in blood crying and I walked over to him and wrapped my body around him. Kai came back with our parents and sisters and they looked at me in horror like they were ashamed that I killed those Lions and saved my brother," he frowns.

I scowl. "Why would they be ashamed of you? You didn't know that you were a Wolf Blood. You felt threatened, and you reacted with your Blood. That's something you couldn't control for the first time, it's an instinct. You saved your brother! That's amazing Noah!" He looks at me then smiles and blushes. "The happiest part of that day was the look in Scout's eyes when I saved him. He was smiling and crying. He was only ten on that day, but he's probably eleven now," he says. "At least you saved your brother; I had a chance to save my sister and I blew it," I frown. "You did save her Kira. She is safe in the next life. I bet she's looking down on us right now," Noah looks up at the sky. I begin to cry and look up at the sky with Noah. *If you can hear me Lily, please watch over us as we travel to the Lion's Kingdom. I know the path will be dangerous.*

The sun peeps out and I stretch my arms out. Noah helps me up and I tap Ethan with my foot. "Let's start traveling," I say. Ethan wakes up and we start walking. We walk in silence for about ten minutes. *Something doesn't feel right.*

The trees are shaking in a different way. I stop moving and place my feet firmly on the ground. "Kira, you ok?" Ethan asks. My body was shaking back and forth, but not purposely. *Oh no, a quake...* "Kira..." Noah looks over at me. *He feels it too, it's not just me.* I look back at him nervously, then start running away quickly. "Kira!!" Noah screams behind me. I lost sight of Ethan, and Noah chases behind me. *Don't worry about Ethan right now, focus on staying alive.* The ground begins to crumble and split apart beneath me and I scream and fall on my knees. Noah screams behind me and I turn around to see him falling in the sinking ground.

"Noah!!!" I scream and look down at him. "Kira!" I hear his voice faintly. I see his body holding onto a small piece of land that was already sinking into the ground. I reach down to grab him and he stretches his hand out to me. The land he was on continues to sink into the ground. He grabs my arm so tightly it hurts and I close my eyes fighting back tears. "Kira look at me!" he yells. I open my eyes with tears forming in them. "You have to get out of here!!" he screams loudly in my ear.

"No I don't want to leave you down there!" I yell back. We both start to fall in the hole when he starts slipping down my arm. "Kira go be safe!! I'll be ok I promise!!" he screams then lets go of my arm and disappears in the deep dark hole. *Stay alive for me please, Noah.* I then listen to him and start running. Snow starts falling lightly. I don't know where to go, but I'm
just going to run. I eventually find a small cave and curl up in there
and fall asleep.

I wake up shaking from the cold. I don't have my blanket. *Bloodshed* still hangs on my hip. My arm scarred up from the cut. I lost my backpack trying to get Noah out of the hole. *Don't worry Noah I'm coming for you. What if something happened to him? What if he escaped? What if he didn't? Ugh, I hate asking "what if" questions. What if he's...dead? Shut up Kira.* He will probably find me again, and so will Ethan. *Ethan, please don't make me assume that you are the stupid Lion I expect you to be and don't betray me. I want to be able to trust you, but I find that hard right now.*

I stand up off the snowy ground and look at the debris around me. Trees collapsed everywhere and holes everywhere in the ground. "Noah! Ethan!" I yell. I call Noah and Ethan's names over and over for hours. No responses, not even a sign a movement. I'm not giving up though. They both know my secret. *I couldn't care less about my secret right now; I just want to survive.* I won't stop until both of them are safe. I just hope they are both alive and breathing right now.

9 NOAH

I open my eyes and look up at the grey sky. Snow sprinkles the ground around me or what's left of the ground. I stand up and my body aches miserably. I grab my shoulder in pain and hiss loudly. I grunt as I brush the debris off of me. The hole I'm in looks deeper than last night when I fell.. The ground still trembles in fear from the quake last night. Snow melts upon my cheek as I scratch the back of my head. I push the nearest tree out of my way and something jingles in my ear. I look underneath the tree and find a small, purple backpack covered in dirt and dust. *Kira… I have to get out of this hole and search for her.*

I sling Kira's backpack over my shoulder and I begin climbing out. I grab a rock and hoist myself up onto another chunk of land. I use the broken trees and rocks to make my way up the steep hole. What felt like an hour later, I manage to pull myself out of the hole. I turn around and gaze at the deep empty crater and shiver slightly as the snow starts to pick up heavily. It looked as if a monster from underground came up and bit off a piece of the land. *How the hell did I manage to survive this? That doesn't matter, right now I need to make sure that Kira is safe.*

I walk for hours and there is still no sign of her. I really hope she's alright. I know that the quake scared her; I could see it in her eyes she was terrified. She is hardly afraid though. She has been aggressive and tough ever since we met, it was frightening to see her scared. It's very weird to see a strong, rough and fearless person cry and be scared like they were never that strong person in the first place. Well, I guess you can't be brave without being scared. Most people can act like it, but some rarely take off the mask and show who they really are inside. I think underneath Kira's brave face is a frightened and emotional girl.

I keep on walking when my ears detect a noise. I mutate into my Wolf Blood and listen closely to the sound. I carry Kira's backpack between my jaws. My paws become damp and colder with every step I take. I lower my nose to the ground and see if I can catch a scent. I inhale deeply, but the deep snow is stuffing up my black nose. I sneeze lightly when the noise becomes louder. I start to pick up the pace and follow the groaning noise. I then stop when I see a person in a cave curled up in a ball.

I walk up to her and she sits there shivering violently with her eyes closed shut. I nudge her with my wet nose and she opens one eye nervously. She must be freezing out here alone in the middle of the cold. I crawl in the space between her and she shakes more. *I'm right here Kira, I'm here for you.* Kira's freezing hands stroke my grey fur as I watch her eyes open slowly. Her quivering lip forms into a smile. I lick her rosy red cheeks and try to warm her up. "N-Noah…" she could barely say. I then crawl away from her and mutate silently. I put the backpack down, take out her blanket, and wrap it around her pale body.

I crouch down next to her and slide my arm around her waist. I pull her body closer to mine and hold her tightly. She puts her cold face against my neck and closes her eyes. I watch as tears slide down her red, puffy cheeks. She wraps her body around mine. "N-N-Noah," she struggles to say. "Shhhh, I'm right here, Kira. Try and get some rest," I tell her. I stroke her hair and her face gently. I look down into her beautiful green eyes and I kiss her cheek. She begins to fall asleep, trembling in my arms.

I watch her silently sleep while I warm her up with my body heat. I hope she didn't catch a cold or something worse from being out here too long. I'll make sure to take care of her and get her better as soon as possible. She's fought through so much already; it would hurt me to have her get sick at all. I stroke her soft brown hair and I hum a gentle tune in her ear. She starts shaking again, so I bend down and kiss her forehead. "Calm down Kira you're ok. I'm here," I whisper in her ear. *I'm here little Tiger, don't worry you're safe.*

She keeps on shivering and I nudge her a little bit to wake her up. She opens her eyes and holds me tight. I could see tears racing down her face. "Kira what's wrong?" I ask worryingly. "I just had a bad dream is all. I'm fine," she says trying to hide her tears. I pull a long string of hair out of her face and put it behind her ear. "I'm here for you don't worry," I say. She nods and looks up at the sky then at me. "Did you see Ethan anywhere?" she sniffles. "No, I'm sorry," I say. *Hahaha, like I would even bother to look for him. We would have been fine if we didn't have to look for him.*

She looks up into my eyes and I look right back at her. *She looks so beautiful when she looks up at me. I feel like she actually cares for me.* I then slowly lean down and kiss her lips lightly. She kisses me back softly then pulls away and closes her eyes. "Did… you not like that?" I ask her. She opens her eyes and chuckles. "I did like that idiot," she nudges me. I giggle and she kisses me one last time. "Let's go and find Ethan," she says and winks at me. She stands up then helps me up on my feet. I hide my frown from her. *Anything for you Kira…Even if it means finding Ethan.*

10 ETHAN

I blink my eyes open slowly as my body surges in pain all around. My memory is a little bit fuzzy. I can't remember the last thing that happened to me. *Who am I? My name is Ethan Kingsley, I am a Prince. I have an older brother named Jett, and my father is the King. What did I do? I left the Kingdom and what was I doing? Hunting? I can't remember.* I try to look around to see if I can make out where I am, but all I see are people blocking my vision.

"Is he dead?" a young voice whispers. "No, I think he's just unconscious," a second voice replies. A cold finger touches my throat. "I can't find a pulse," a man says. "Wait, his chest is moving!!" a female gasps when multiple arms grab me. I groan and try to move my body upward. "Ethan? Prince Ethan?" a male voice asks me. "Huh?" I ask him. "He's alive!! Somebody help me get him to a doctor, quick!" the man yells when three or four men help me shuffle my way towards the infirmary.

The doctor touches my shoulder and I wince in pain. "Hmm, you have some bad bruising in a few places. We will just have to wait until it heals," the doctor tells me. "Do you remember anything before waking up Prince Ethan?" he asks. "No," I say. He touches my head and I wince in pain. "You may have a mild concussion, as well. I suggest you just try and get some rest, but don't sleep with a concussion. It could give you more problems later on," the male doctor says. He moves my hair aside to look at the back of my head. "You don't seem to be bleeding, which is good," he says. I groan and place my hand on my forehead. "Can I leave?" I ask him. "You may in a few minutes. The kingdom is happy to see you alive and well Prince Ethan," the doctor smiles. *Not everyone.*

The doctor gives me some medicine and I relax on the table. My head thumps loudly when I suddenly feel my memory piecing together. *The quake. Kira and*

Noah separated from me and I got hit in the head with something. I remember the sound of Lion's running and roaring and then I blacked out. It wasn't long when the King walks into the doctor's room. "Nice for you to join us again," he says mockingly. "What do you want?" I ask him.

"To refresh your memory. What did I tell you last time you were down here?" he asks me. *You threatened to kill me if I didn't kill Kira and Noah.* "You told me to kill the Bloods that I was traveling with," I say. "Yes. I am glad that the quake separated you. I hope that your friends died in the quake because you can't even do that apparently. The next time when they get close, I will personally go out and kill the both of them and bring you their heads," he says angrily.

I stand up and my father grabs my arm tightly and drags me out the door. "Hey, wait! Sir, you can't take my patient out. He needs to stay in here and rest," the doctor says. "He can rest in his new room," my father says and walks me down the hall. *New room?* He pulls out something metal and he clicked it around my wrist. *A bracelet? Why did he give me a bracelet?* We stop all of a sudden and my father shoves me in a rusty cell. There was only a dirty bed with a ripped up blanket and bloody walls.

"What the hell?" I scream. "This is your punishment for not following my orders. You trying to be friends with outsiders is as crazy as your mother trying to make peace!!" he yells. I growl and try to step out of the room when shocking fills my body. I fall backwards and squirm on the floor. "You'll never be able to get out. Your bracelet makes you incapable of mutating and escaping from the jail cell. I paid your weapons designer friend to design those. Welcome home, son," my father laughs then leaves me in pain.

How the hell am I supposed to get out of here now? With this bracelet on me it's impossible to escape. The only two ways I could get out of here is if someone deactivates the bracelet, or if I could break it somehow. He said Chase designed these, so maybe he knows how to shut it off. I bet Kira could break it; she's the strongest person I know. I hope Kira is doing alright. I would kill my father if it meant being with Kira right now.

I lay in my cell for a few hours trying not to sleep like the doctor said. "Hey idiot," a voice disturbs my thoughts. I look up into the dark eyes of my older brother Jett who is smiling from ear to ear. He unlocks my door and stands back. "Dad wants to show you something," he laughs.

I try to step out, but I get instantly shocked throughout my whole body. I fall back and sit in the corner of my cell shaking crazily.

"Whoops, guess I forgot to turn off the shock field," he says sarcastically. *Asshole*. He then flips a switch to his right and the bracelet beeped twice. I step out weakly and avoid making eye contact with him. He then put his arm out in front of me to stop me from walking. "Oh and dad told me to tell you this," he pauses. He grabs me by the shirt and brings me closer to his face. "If you try to escape at all, he'll kill you before you can call your friends to help," he growls deeply. His breath stinks of bloody meat and wine. "Ok…" I cough out and he drops me on the floor roughly. *Guess I will have to escape while they are asleep*. We then slowly walk towards the throne room where my father was waiting for me.

The laughter of my father alarms me. I look up and he turns around his chair to face me. "Ah my son just in time. I want to show you a fun video," he says laughing. I bite my lip and look down at the wooden floor. "So…you interrupted my rest to watch one of your stupid cameras?" I ask him. "Oh not just any video. I think you'll *love* this particular video my cameras caught," he laughs. I sit down in the closest leather chair to me and two large guards stand behind me.

My father turns on the camera and the first thing I see is myself. I was hitting the camera with a stone and the camera shut off. My father plants hidden cameras everywhere. They are disguised as plants, rocks, or bark in trees. I destroyed quite a few while I was out there with Kira and Noah. I wanted to make sure he didn't see where I was taking Kira and Noah so that he wouldn't send out guards to kidnap them. The thought of him watching not just me, but harmless Bloods walking around makes me want to throw up. I look over to see my dad staring at me. "I want to show you my favorite part," he says then switches cameras. The second camera shows the quake splitting Noah, Kira, and I up. I look to the ground, close my eyes, and growl under my breath.

"Kira, Shhhh you're ok now..." the monitor speaks. I look up instantly and my stomach drops to the floor. Noah holds Kira in his arms as she shook violently, helpless. I fight the tears forming in my eyes. She starts crying and she says his name lightly. I watch as Noah strokes her hair gently and he holds her tight. He then leans into her then...no. "No!! No!! NO!!!' I scream loudly then stand up quickly. I bang my fist on the table twice then climb up and walk closer to the camera. "I should be the one holding her and kissing her!!!!!" I yell to the camera. I angrily hit the camera with my fist and I rip out the cords and smash it to the floor. My knuckles start to bleed from the glass, and I kick the camera twice then the guards grab my arms.

"Well isn't this precious, you're in love with this poor girl," my father laughs. "Yes I'm in love with her, and you're not going to stop me from seeing her!!" I scream at him. "Well, let's just see if I can say...hmmm...arrange a visit with these two. I would love to meet this special girl that you like so much," he laughs. The guards begin to drag me out of the room. "LISTEN TO ME YOU BEAST, YOU HURT A HAIR ON HER HEAD YOU'RE DEAD!!! DEAD!!" I scream angrily. The guards place me back in my cell. I take a minute to calm down, and I sit on my bed to think to myself.

Kira would put up a good fight against my dad. Ugh, I can't even call him my dad anymore. He sickens me to no end. I swear when I have the chance, I will kill him. With all the strength I have, I would gladly strangle the life out of him just like he is doing with my life. I can't put up with all the shit that he's doing. Killing innocent Bloods, murdering his own wife for speaking out and wanting to have peace, putting his own son on lockdown. He knows I'm against him.

He has always picked Jett over me because he's older and he agrees with everything that dad says. Jett is dumber than a rock. While my father has an army, I have a bigger weapon that can't be beat. A White Tiger Blood. The *last* Tiger Blood standing on this world. She's on my side; she has the same mind as I do. She reminds me of my own mother. She's so sweet and innocent like mother was until dad killed her. I'm just glad that Kira is safe right now. Despite Noah kissing her, she's safe.

11 KIRA

I wake up in a cold tree with a warm body pressed up against mine. *How did I get in a tree? Wasn't I in a cave?* My memory has gone to rust since the quake. I'm not even sure what has happened in the past twenty-four hours. After the quake, I ended up freezing cold from the snow; I couldn't move a finger. My head throbbed and hurt a lot while I was alone. The only part I remember was when Noah found me. *I do remember a Wolf Blood coming into the cage. What other Wolf do I know besides Noah?* Normally, I have the best memory ever. I could remember stuff back when I was two years old. Now I can't quite picture it quite as well as I could before. I also remember when Noah kissed me.

I'm not even sure that I have feelings for him at all. *Well maybe I do.* I do remember kissing him back though. Noah is very sweet and kind, but he is also a big distraction for me. He can get to be a real pain in my ass, yet he is quite helpful at times. Guys can be stupid and annoying though. All I know is that Noah really cares for me and he is loyal and protective. *Unlike Ethan who keeps disappearing. Do I have feelings for Noah? And if I do, what feelings? I trust him; he is helpful; and he is very passionate towards me.*

Oh Ethan, I hope he's safe. *I hope he isn't doing anything stupid.* Splitting up like this makes me really nervous. I know being the most powerful Blood in the world should be all about being fearless and strong, but I'm not like that at all. I get nervous and frightened a lot. *Ethan better be loyal and keep his mouth shut.* I may not show my emotions much, but I do feel fear. Everyone feels emotions differently. Fear, love, hatred, happiness—any emotion—everyone feels things differently.

It doesn't matter if I am the most powerful, most intelligent, or wealthiest Blood in the world, we all feel emotions differently. My fear is losing my family. I already lost my mother, father, and sister tragically, but to me, there is family all around. Noah and Ethan, maybe other people we meet on the way, everyone is *my* family, and family sticks together through tough times.

I stretch my arms out and look down at the ground. I look over and catch Noah watching me. "What are you looking at?" I ask. "I'm looking at you, silly. Sorry we are in a tree, but the snow started falling quickly and we were getting snowed in the cave. I left you sleeping and dug us out then carried you up into this tree. The snow died down after that. Did you know you are a really deep sleeper? It's interesting," Noah smiles. "I slept through all of that?" I gasp. Noah nods. "That's alright, you looked adorable sleeping, but are you feeling alright now?" he asks. "Yes, I feel better. I think we better get traveling soon before the snow starts falling again," I say. "Hold on let me jump down first," he says.

Noah jumps down steadily and brushes off a few leaves from his clothes. "Let me help you down little Tiger," Noah says. "Alright, you helped me once Noah and I thank you for that, but you don't need to go all out for me. I can handle myself. Just like you said, I'm a little Tiger. Tigers are strong and powerful," I laugh. "Yes, but this certain little Tiger was weak and cold when I found her. Therefore, I will help this little Tiger until she is better. Please, let me help you," he says. I giggle then hop down. Noah catches me then places me on the ground. "Thank you Noah," I look
up at him. He leans in and kisses my head lightly. "No problem little Tiger," he smiles.

We walk for about an hour when I don't recognize the area around us. "Noah?" I ask him. He turns to face me. "Yes, what is it? Are you ok? Do you need anything?" he asks rather quickly. "I was just going to ask if you know where we are going," I say and chuckle. "Ummmm....Maybe?" he says. I laugh at him and I stop walking. "You have no idea!!" I say hysterically. "Alright miss Tiger Blood, then *you* tell me where to go," he says sarcastically. "Alright, and don't call me a Tiger Blood so loudly. There could be somebody listening to us," I say.

We have been walking all day without knowing where to go, fantastic. I nudge him out of the way and I feel the ground beneath my feet. I look around and notice the grass seems greener than they should be. *The plants should be turning brown when it gets cold, especially the grass.* I bend down and rub some grass lightly. "This feels a bit strange. I feel as if we are so close, but I can't put my finger on it," I say looking at the grass under me.

"Here how about we stop for the night ok? You need rest. You hit your head pretty hard when I found you," Noah says then taps my forehead lightly. "Wait... I hit my head?" I ask him. "Yeah, don't you remember? You started mumbling strange things as you slept. You have a little bump right here," he says and digs his fingers through my hair. He stops and put his index finger on a swollen part of my head. I touch that part and throb in pain as I touch it. "So *that's* why I'm having trouble remembering stuff," I sigh loudly and Noah puts his finger on my chin and raises my head. "Hey, you're fine now and we found each other again. That's all that matters," he says smiling reassuringly.

"I guess we can stop and take a break," I say. We keep walking until we find a nice, open field of grass. I get on my back and look up at the stars. Noah does the same thing and he puts his arm around my waist. *The stars are shining brightly tonight. I wish I could go up and see the stars.* "Hey Noah?" He turns to me. "Yeah?" he replies. "Do you ever think that there could be other Bloods out there beyond the stars?" I ask. "Well, there *could* be other creatures out there. I don't know if they would be Bloods like us. Why do you ask?" he says. "I don't know I'm just curious." I say.

I turn to face him and I look into his light brown eyes then he smiles. He kisses my lips softly then backs away. "Do you remember that from last night?" he asks me. "Yes, I do remember that," I say and smile. We kiss once more then I wrap my arms around him. "Goodnight my little Tiger," he says then kisses my forehead. *Maybe I do like Noah. He hasn't done anything for me to doubt him.* I say nothing but bury my face in the crook of his neck and fall asleep very quickly.

I wake with a cold shiver down my spine. I crawl away from sleeping Noah, and I stand up and stretch my arms out above my head. I turn around when something catches my eye. I walk over to a green bush, and I touch the leaves lightly. *Huh, this bush is darker than the one next to it.* I step into the darker bush when my foot sinks into the ground. *What? Why is there a hole underneath this bush?* I groan loudly, and Noah wakes up. "Kira?" he asks. "Noah help me I'm stuck!" I yell at him. He stands up quickly and runs over to help. He grabs my waist and pulls me out of the bush.

I pant softly and he looks at me curiously. "What happened?" he asks. "I was just looking at this strange bush and I fell into it. I think there's a hole under the bush," I explain to him. He walks over to the bush and he looks into it. "This bush is artificial," he tells me. "I thought it looked different. Who would make a fake bush though?" I ask.

"I don't know. We live in a world of forests and lakes, it doesn't make sense for someone to make fake trees and bushes," he says. He picks up the fake bush and pushes it aside. A large deep hole appears beneath it. "What do you think is down there?" Noah asks me. *I don't know but I want to find out.* "Let's find out," I say and stick my feet down in the hole. I grab my sword and sling it around my shoulder.

"Whoa hold on, hun. We don't know what's down there," he says worried. *That's why we go down into the hole and find out dumbass.* He places his hand on my shoulder and I look up at him annoyed. "Kira, I can't stand to lose you again," he says. "C'mon Noah, I feel very confident about this just trust me," I say. He blinks his eyes and shakes his head. "No, I'm not letting you down there."

He crosses his arms. I roll my eyes at him then crawl down the hole. "Kira!!!" He screams angrily. I laugh and fall down smoothly in the dark hole. *Sorry Noah. My curiosity is getting the best of me.* I look around and see lightly lit torches along the walls of this underground cave. *Huh, why are there torches in a hole underground? Is someone else down here?*

I listen as Noah falls down the hole after me. He stands up and brushes dirt off of him. "Kira, why don't you listen to me? You could get hurt. We don't know what could be down here," he says angrily. I hear voices talking in the distance and I stop to look down the tunnel. "Are you even listening to me??" Noah grabs my shoulder. "Shhhh, shut up!!" I whisper to him. I look down the tunnel and Noah grabs my hand tightly. I look to him and he gives me a stern look. "Don't let go of my hand, I'm not leaving you here alone in a dark tunnel," he whispers. "Fine," I say. We walk down the hallway, hand in hand.

We walk for a short amount of time when we reach the end of the tunnel. *So the hole under the fake bush leads to an underground tunnel, which leads to a dead end?* People walk by from left and right in different paths. A few people stop and stare at Noah and I curiously. A man whispers to the woman next to her and she nods then runs off. *Who are these people and why do they live underground?* Other people glare and give Noah and I eerie looks. "Kira…" Noah says softly.

I turn and see two large men in armor heading straight for us. Noah steps in front of me then mutates. "Noah kill them!" I yell before he attacks the two men. I take *Bloodshed* out of her case and quickly follow the two men and Noah. I finally reach them when four arms grab my body. I turn around to the men, and I swing my sword sharply cutting off their fingers. I laugh as they shriek in pain.

More strong men try to grab me, but I quickly stab them in the chest. The other men flee along with the rest of the people. I turn around and see Noah hiding in a corner. I grab him by his fur and pull him out of the corner, and he winces in pain. "Come on Noah we have to follow them!!" I scream at him. His ears fall down and he whimpers. I start walking and he limps behind me. All of a sudden Noah barks and I turn to see that he was being taken away by more guards. "Noah!!" I yell and run back. I lost sight of him when three men startled me and I drop my sword. I squirm and shake but they had a tight grip on me.

Mutate Kira mutate! Kill them before they kill you! They soon stop and open a shiny silver door and walk into a dark room. They drop me on the floor then close the door behind them. *Don't mutate. They might kill me. Control yourself and don't be stupid.* I hear a loud groan and human Noah steps out from the darkness. I run over and he wraps his arms around me tightly. He kisses my forehead then my lips then he backs away. "I'm sorry Kira…" he whispers in my ear. "No it's my fault, I should have listened to you. I didn't know it was dangerous down here," I say. He runs his hands down my back when the door opens again. A tall figure walks in the room chuckling.

61

"Hello, isn't it nice for you to join us down here in the Lion's Kingdom," the deep raspy voice says. *Wait, the Lion's Kingdom has been underground this whole time? How is that even possible?* I look up at him, but I can't see his face clearly. The lights then turn on brightly. "My name is Andrew," he says then holds out a hand to me. *Go fuck yourself King Andrew.* I stare at him and grit my teeth. I spit on the ground in front of him and growl deeply as Noah pulls me back.

"Why are we locked up?" Noah asks. "Well, I would like to know who our mysterious guests are who came in and started killing my people," Andrew says. "I'm Noah, and I'm a Wolf Blood." Andrew nods then walks closer to me. He examines my frail body and chuckles to himself. "And who's this lovely young woman?" He asks. I look him straight in the eyes and frown. "No one of *your* concern," I say.

"Well, I believe this is my concern. I don't want two rebels in my kingdom," he says. "We aren't rebels," I say. *That's a lie, we are technically rebels.* "Hmm, well you certainly are a special girl aren't you?" he laughs. *Special is one way to put it.* "Fuck off," I say sharply. "Kira be polite. He is a King," Noah whispers behind me. "Oh I'm so sorry, *please* fuck off your royal highness," I say again then bow to him. "Kira!" Noah snaps. The man grabs my arm and brings me closer to him.

"A little snippy now are we young lady?" he laughs. I pull my arm away. "Don't touch me," I say. He takes a step back and continues laughing. "You better start being more respectful sweetheart. You *are* talking to a King. If you want to survive here you both will listen to me and behave. Another one of those outbursts and I'll cut that pretty little tongue out," he laughs then locks the door behind him. "King Asshole. That should be your new nickname," I whisper to myself before Noah and I went to sleep.

12 ETHAN

"Chase!! Chase!!" I whisper through the thick metal bars of my cell. He glances at me nervously then walks away. *Huh? Why would he leave me here? I thought he was my best friend. Maybe my dad told him not to talk to me, don't overthink it.* I lay back in my bed and crawl under my blanket. Another cold night alone in this prison cell. I close my eyes and I think of Kira. I swear even if my dad hurts her a little bit, I'll kill him. I sit up on my bed and I take my knife out and hold it firmly. *I could stab my father with this.* I giggle softly to myself and put the shiny blade back in my pocket. *Is it wrong to kill my own father? Probably. Is it wrong to kill innocent bloods who've done nothing wrong just for power? Absolutely.*

It drives me insane that somehow I'm related to that manipulative-demented asshole. Being his son is probably the worst thing I could be. I would rather be his nephew or his cousin, but no, I had to be his son. *I would rather not be related to him at all, but I can't change that. I was born into this family and I can't be un-born into the family. I think mom was the lucky one in this family. She didn't have to suffer the rage of my father that I am dealing with right now. She is calm and peaceful in the next life; maybe she's even looking down on me. I hope she is watching over Kira and giving her strength.*

I hope Kira can fight. She's aggressive, and I think she can handle herself. I still want to protect her though. I mean who knows what my father will do if he finds out she's a Tiger. *He might know already. He has those cameras hidden all over Bitotem. He doesn't usually look at the cameras unless there is a threat. Unless someone really pays attention to those cameras, I don't think he knows about Kira.* He'll do anything in his crazy mind to kill her. I won't let him though. I'd rather be killed than watch Kira be tortured. I finally make a decision on what to do. "I will kill my father and end this war," I whisper to myself.

I plot out a plan in my head perfectly. *First, I ask my dad to let me go and I'll tell him that I'll kill Kira and Noah. Second, I find them and tell them to run away. Third step, Kira breaks the bracelet off of me so I can escape. Finally, I'll use my blade to kill my father in great defeat.* "Hehehe," I giggle. Now for phase one. "Hello! Dad! Jett?" I shout. I only hear my echo scream back at me. "Hello! Guards! Somebody?" I scream once again. Nobody responds to me and I bang my bracelet against the metal bars and make a loud clunking sound. I then hear stomping footsteps walking towards me.

"Quit making noises!" A guard screams at me. "Could you do me a grateful honor of getting the King for me, sir? I would like to speak to him," I ask him. "Will you shut up if I do?" He grumbles. "Yes, I will I promise," I say and give him a smile. "Fine," he groans then left. About five minutes later, my father storms up to my cell. "What do you want?" he grumbles. "I have a proposal I think you may be interested in," I say. "I'm listening," he says. "Do you want those two bloods down here in the next twenty-four hours?" I ask him. He looks at me suspiciously. He smiles for a minute then it quickly wipes away. "I want their heads chopped off and then sewn back on together," he laughs. I swallow nervously.

"For my release from this bracelet, I'll bring the Wolf Blood and the other girl here by tomorrow," I say. "Eh so? What's in it for me son?" he asks. "You didn't let me finish father," I say politely. He squints at me then breathes in sharply. "Go on," he says. "I will kill them in front of you and the whole kingdom. If that will win back your trust, I will do it," I say bravely. He looks at me and smiles. "Now there's the son I know!" he says excitedly. He presses the button by the door to release me and I walk out. "Before you go, stand right here, and close your eyes. I have something to give you," he says. *This can't be good. He will probably do something horrible to me. I have to listen to him though or he will kill me.*

I respectfully obey and close my eyes. I hear the sound of metal clanging against the ground. *Crap. That sounds like a weapon.* I try to ignore it and stand still. All of a sudden, I feel a sharp pain slice straight through my shirt. Pain swarms my chest and warm blood runs down my body. "Dahhh!" I shriek and fall down on the ground. I open my eyes and my father grabs my bloody shirt and pins me against the hard brick wall. I open my eyes and watch the blood drip down my chest. He throws me in my cell and I wince in pain on the floor.

"Do you think I'm an idiot boy? The minute I let you step out of this Kingdom, you will run off with that little bitch and never come back. Whether you like me or not, you are my son and I will not have my son disrespect me and his Kingdom," he growls. I glance over at the weapon he used to attack me. The bloody sword sits on the ground and I stare at it carefully. The sword shines brighter than the blood shed on it.

That sword looks familiar. My father slaps me hard across the face. "Don't you dare think you can get out of here easily like that!" My father threatens. He stands up, closes the door and lock it up. I shake violently and I hold my chest with my left arm. "Oh relax it's just a paper cut," my dad laughs. I crawl over to the entrance and I watch my dad clean the sword with a towel then he hands the sword to one of his guards. I swallow deeply and sit in the back of my cell in pain.

My dad fixes his collar and stomps out of the room. Not only did my own father strike me, but he did it with Kira's sword. *What is he doing with Bloodshed? If he has Kira's sword then he has Kira. Shit.* Kira is here somewhere too. I don't know if that's good or bad. I slowly climb up on my uncomfortable bed and shake, blood spilling everywhere I go. I rest my thumping head on my pillow and try my best not to cry. *Oh Kira. If you and Noah are here, please be safe. Don't piss off my father, or he will just torture you. Be smart about what you say and do, Kira or you might get killed.*

I squirm around in my bed for the next few hours. I cover up my wound with my blanket and try to apply pressure to it. I whimper loudly and a tear runs down my cheek. I call for help, but no one hears me. *Or they are ignoring me.* I then sit there waiting for my seventeen years of my not so wonderful life to flash by me. Just then I hear someone unlock my door and I look up at the person. "Chase!" I say loudly. He puts a finger to his mouth telling me to be quiet. He then takes a bottle of water and pours it on my wound.

He takes out a white cloth and he wraps it tightly around my wound. I wince slightly as he focuses on my chest. He tapes up the cloth then he steps out silently. He locks the jail cell and glares at me for a second. "I'm so sorry Ethan," he whispers then disappears. *Thank you for helping me Chase. I know you probably have orders not to talk to prisoners.* I can feel my wound starting to heal already. I lay back and try to catch up on sleeping.

13 KIRA

I couldn't sleep at all; I keep walking around in a circle with my head thumping loudly. I'm just so angry that I could kill someone right now. Not only do I have to fight for myself against Andrew, but I have to protect Noah's life as well and find Ethan's life. *If Ethan's still alive.* I suddenly feel an arm grab my leg and I fall down on my knees. I look over to my leg and shake it off. "Noah let go!!!" I yell. He releases my leg but then tackles me, wraps his arms around my waist playfully and holds me in place. I squirm in his arms. I try to scream, but he covers my mouth with his hand. I bite and lick his hand trying to free myself, but he just sits there motionless.

"Bite all you want sweetie; I'm not letting you go," he says. I wiggle around a little bit and he chuckles at me. I then give up and sit there, defeated. I mumble angrily and he kisses my head gently. "Kira, listen to me. I'm frustrated too, but if we want to get out of here alive then we will have to cooperate with the King. I know you don't like him, but we have to cooperate," he says. *You're wrong, I hate King Asshole. I want to stab my sword through his heart and watch his life bleed out in front of me.* I groan loudly, then I look up into his brown eyes and nod in agreement. His hand still covers my mouth. "Now I'm going to take my hand off and let you go. Will you behave?" he asks me. I nod again and he smiles. "Good," He says then slowly moves his hand from my mouth.

I sit there slowly breathing in and out. "Good girl, now let's get some sleep, okay?" he says and runs his fingers through my curly hair. I kiss his cheek and he kisses my lips softly. "How about a few more minutes, hmm? I'm not feeling sleepy yet," I say and he chuckles. "I'm fine with that," he says then climbs on top of me. We kiss passionately and I moan softly. He moves my hair back and he pecks my neck with kisses. A strange feeling moves around in my stomach and I squirm around. *What was that? That felt weird.*

We continue kissing when the strange feeling turns in my stomach again. *Listen to your body Kira, something doesn't feel right.* "You ok?" he asks. "Yeah I just don't know if I am ready for all of this yet. I don't want to rush into a relationship when we are prisoners. King Asshole is probably waiting to find out what Blood I am before killing us. I don't think doing this is good for a time like this. Let's wait until we escape from here," I tell him. He got up and moves off of me. "That's ok I won't rush you. Just tell me when you are ready," he says and kisses my lips once more before I cuddle into his warm body and start to dream.

The scents of grass and roses fill my nostrils. I blink my eyes and look out into the open field. In the middle of the tall grass stands Ethan waving for me to come over. I run to him wearing shorts and a blue t-shirt. He plays with my brown curly hair and starts tickling me all over. "Hehehe Ethan stop!" I yell. He then continues to tickle me. We run around and chase each other through the open fields, into a dark forest, and finally stop at a crystal clear lake where both Ethan and I begin to swim. After playing in the water for a little while, we set up a campfire and relax.

I look up into his handsome grey eyes and smile. He smiles back and we come together in a long kiss. My vision gets blurry and I feel my body shake a little. "Kira wake up!" Noah's voice echoes in my dream. I blink my eyes rapidly and wake up from my dream. "C'mon little Tiger, the King requires us to be in his throne room right now. I think he is serving us breakfast," Noah explains. I stretch my arms above my head and Noah helps me stand up. "I'd rather go back into my dream land," I yawn. "I know me too, but let's get this over with," he says. "Alright, and don't call me little Tiger so loudly. I don't know if Andrew has cameras watching us," I say.
"Okay," he replies.

We are escorted into this enormous room with a large table and sit down in comfortable leather seats. We sit there for about five minutes when a tall man walks in the room dressed in all black with spiky hair. "The King will be with you shortly," he says in a deep, boring voice looking at us angrily. I glance over at Noah and his eyes are closed. I tap him on the hand and he opens his eyes. He sighs then winks at me. I suddenly feel a little bit disgusted at him, but I'm not sure why. I mean he's been very helpful with me on this trip. *Maybe I'm getting tired of him. Or maybe it was because of last night. I'm not sure what feeling that was but it didn't feel good when we were kissing.* Loud footsteps echo in the room and disrupt my thoughts. The King sits down in the largest chair in the room and stares at the both of us.

It stays silent for a minute when I speak out. "What are you looking at you beast?" I snap. He looks at me with no reaction and blinks his eyes. "A sharp witted girl who's going to get a limb chopped off next time she makes a smart remark," he says. *That doesn't matter. I could still kill you with one arm or one leg. It would be harder to mutate though.* I clench my fist and bite my tongue, trying not to say anything else. "Now that that's settled, how about some breakfast?" he says. I say nothing and he snaps his fingers. About ten or twelve people come out and place food on the table.

Eggs, ham, bread, bacon. Almost every breakfast food I can think of is being placed in front of me. Milk, potatoes, and many other kinds of delicious food. My stomach growls at me ready to eat, but my minds disagree. *This has to be some sort of trick. I bet all of this food is poisonous.* "Eat up you two," King Andrew says. Noah smiles widely and digs in and eats like a slob. *You tell me to be respectful towards a King yesterday, then eat like a caveman who hasn't seen food in a year the next day in front of him? Come on, Noah.*

I stare at the steaming sausages in front of me. My mouth waters and my stomach growls. I want to eat, but something inside of me tells me not to. It just doesn't make any sense on what he's trying to do. I mean does he think we are going to respect him if he gives us food? Is he trying to fatten us up then kill us? Noah and I came in here, killed four of his guards, and then he threw us in a cold room. Now, the next morning he is serving us breakfast? "Why aren't you eating sweetheart?" he says staring at me across the table. "I'm not hungry," I tell him. *I'm fucking starving; I haven't eaten in three days!* He looks me in the eye then slowly took a bite of some ham and sausage. "So tell me, how did you two get down here?" Andrew asks. He looks towards Noah, but his mouth is full, so I have to do all of the talking. "Well, I fell into a hole behind a dark bush, which I realized it was fake, and I was curious on what was down here," I tell him. He smirks at me. Noah gulps down his food. "And I followed her because I have to protect her," Noah groans out. I stomp on his foot under the table. "Ow!" He screams. He looks at me questionably and I give him an angry look.

"Protect her? Now why is that?" he asks. "No big reason. He is just bound to protect me as he would protect a loved one. Just his typical Wolf Blood instincts," I answer. "Hmm, are you some sort of *special* Blood sweetheart?" He asks me. "No, I haven't discovered my Blood yet, sir. I am still very young," I lied. *I'm more powerful than all your Lions combined.* "Hmm, alright," he says. I sit up in my chair. "So sweetheart, is there anything you desire? Anything you want in this world?" he asks me. *Yes, I would love to put my sword through your neck.*

I open my mouth getting ready to say something when it hit me. *He's not just being nice to us; instead, he's trying to get us on his side by bribing us with food and goods. I need to look for a way to escape here.* "Actually there is sir," I say and smile at him. "And what might that be?" he asks. "I would love to see more of this...mysterious hidden kingdom of yours. Might I have a tour?" I tell him politely. He looks at me for a minute. "An odd request, why do you want to see the Kingdom?" he asks. "I'm just very curious and this is the first Kingdom I've been in and I just want to see it," I say. "Very well," he says then snaps his fingers. The same man in black comes out and grabs my arm.

"My name is Jett, and I'm the King's son," he says. I smile at him. "It's nice to meet you Jett," I say and hold out my hand. *Perfect. Now I know who to kill next after Andrew.* He shakes it firmly and we stare at each other for a minute. *Huh, he looks a little like Ethan. Weird.* "Over here is where the majority of the Lions live," he says and points to a large opening where Lions were fluently walking in and out. I nod and we keep on walking. "In there is where our head weapons maker is working currently," he says and I see a man hitting a sword with a hammer. *Maybe I could ask him to make me a new sword since King Asshole took mine.* "Cool," I say watching the sword closely.

We walk past some jail cells and I stop. "Who are they?" I ask. "Ugh, just filthy prisoners. Nothing to worry about. Let's keep walking," he says and growls. The third cell is dripping with blood. A man crawls up to the entrance and looks at me curiously. He coughs up a little blood then he smiles. "Kira…" he whispers. I give him a puzzling look when I realize who it is. *Ethan? What is he doing in a jail cell? And why is he bleeding so much?* "Come on let's keep moving," Jett says then grabs my arm tightly and pulls me away. "Wait, Prince Jett! I want to see the prisoners," I say. "No you can't; there's a strict policy about talking to the prisoners. They are dangerous and stupid. Why would you even want to talk to them in the first place?" He says. *I want to talk to Ethan. He shouldn't be a prisoner.*

We keep on walking when Jett opens a door and I follow him inside. The room was pitch black until he turns on the lights. There is a large bed in the room with a window and a large box next to the bed. "What's your name again?" he asks me. "Kira…" I say slowly. "Kira," he repeats. "That's a beautiful name. Why don't you hop on the bed and get comfortable," he says. *What? Get on the bed? Remember what Noah said Kira, just cooperate with them.* I walk over to the bed and sit on it. "What is this room?" I ask. "Oh umm it's just a guest room," he says. He takes something out of the box then walks over to me. He hides the item behind his back and he smiles at me and holds my face in his hand then slides his hand down to my neck. I slowly back away.

"You are a really pretty girl you know that?" he compliments. "Ummmm thanks?" I say nervously. He then climbs on the bed and pushes me down. He handcuffs my left arm to the bed and he gets really close to me. *What the fuck is he doing?* He touches my stomach and moves his hand down my body. He takes my jeans off and I attempt to kick him. "What are you…" I say. He places his finger on my mouth. "Shhh, no talking Kira," he just laughs. "So… my father wants me get some answers from you. I thought the best way to get answers is to torture you, so let's start. What Blood are you?" he asks. "Nothing that you or your father need to know," I snap at him.

He takes off his black belt then hits me on my thighs twice leaving bright red marks. "Wrong answer," he says as I flinch. *That hurt a lot. Doesn't matter what Noah says, I'm not cooperating with this bullshit.* "What are you planning on doing in the Kingdom?" he asks. "N-nothing," I lie. He climbs on top of me and grabs my neck with his hand. He squeezes lightly and I choke a little. "You know I can sense when you are lying Kira. If you lie to me again, I won't be

71

so easy on you," he whispers. I suddenly kick him between his legs and I try to un-handcuff myself. He winces in pain for a minute.

"Oh no, you're not getting away from me that easily," he growls and nips at my neck. I take my right arm and grab his throat. "No, you fucking listen to me. I don't know what you and your demented dad are trying to do to manipulate me, but attempting to rape and torture me will do nothing but make me even more aggressive," I scream in his face. I squeeze my hand harder around his neck. My fingernails become claws and I quickly change back before he realizes. *I want to mutate in self defense, but I can't right now.* I growl lightly and he tries to escape me. *Try not to growl around them. They might suspect I'm a Tiger.*

"Now when I let go, you are going to get the key to the handcuffs, let me go and take me back to my room. Unless you want me to squeeze your neck until your eyes pop out of your head," I offer as I squeeze harder on his neck. He shakes his head. I let him go and he heaves and coughs loudly. He crawls over to the box and took out the key. He hands it to me, and I freed myself. I pull my jeans back on and Jett stands up and waddles over to the door. I hold the metal key in my hand and he opens the door for me. He controls his breathing and he grabs my arm and pulls me close to him. "Don't say a word about this to anyone or I'll come after you and finish up," he growls angrily in my ear. "Oh, I would never embarrass a Prince like that," I say sarcastically and he walks me back to the dinner room.

"Oh there you two are! How was your tour?" King Andrew says. "It was interesting, I love your Kingdom. Very unusual, but delightful," I say with a smile. Jett looks to the ground nervously. "Son is everything alright?" Andrew asks in a rather gloomy tone and glares at him. "Yeah," he grumbles. I look around and notice that Noah is gone. "Where's Noah?" I ask. "He went back to the room. He wasn't feeling well," Andrew says. "Can I go back to my room as well?" I ask politely.

"Of course. Jett would you mind taking her back?" he asks. Jett grumbles and he walks me back to my room. We stop and I look up at him. "Thank you for the tour," I say and smile. He nods. I look around us to make sure that we were alone. "Oh wait, one more thing," I say. He raises an eyebrow. "You can have your key back," I say and stab it into his leg. He shrieks and blood races down his leg. "You little bitch," he cries out. "Have a nice day Jett," I smile and walk back into my room.

14 NOAH

The door creaks open loudly and I can hear a person cry in pain outside. The door slams shut and I hear footsteps walking towards my cold body. "Noah…" Kira whimpers. My eyes struggle to open. She shakes my body and I sit up. "Kira is there something wrong?" I ask her. "Yes, these Bloods here are insane. That guy dressed in all black, he tortured me and tried to rape me. He said King Andrew wanted me tortured to get answers out of me," she says quietly. "What?? I'll kill him," I say angrily. "No, I probably will kill him before you do," she says and lightly chuckles. She then looks to the ground and starts to shake. I wrap my arms around her and hold her tightly.

"What did you do when he tried to touch you?" I ask curiously. "Well, he handcuffed me first then touched me. He asked me what Blood I was and I lied to him. After I lied, he whipped me with his belt he asked me more questions and I still wouldn't answer him, so he touched me. I kicked him then I threatened him that I would kill him. Then he let me go and took me back here to the room then I…" she pauses. "Then you what?" I ask hoping she will continue. "I stabbed him with the key he used to handcuff me to the bed with ," she says then grins. I couldn't help but laugh when she says that. "Kira…" I say.

 "Look I'm sorry Noah, and I know you are probably disappointed in me. I just sort of reacted. I was scared," she says.

"I know, you did well, but you are acting too strong," I tell her.

She looks at me confusingly. "You are acting like a Tiger," I whisper. "Noah I *am* a Tiger, how do you expect me to act?" She asks. "I know, and honestly, I'm impressed how you handled that situation, but if you keep acting like this they are going to catch on that you are a Tiger," I explain. She sighs loudly.

"I guess you're right, again," she giggles lightly. "Do me a favor and take off that brave mask of yours and let out all those feelings underneath. Show them you are just a Blood like everyone else. If they see your emotions, maybe they will let us go, or hopefully not kill us. It would help you if you at least try for me," I kiss her cheek and hold her close to my body. "Oh fine. I'll try and act wimpy just for you, but it won't be any fun," she says. I laugh and stroke her hair gently.

"I saw Ethan locked up in a jail cell, and he was bleeding really badly," she says. I groan irritated and I stand up. "Kira, he is a Lion. We could be up in the world right now roaming, or doing whatever we want, but because of him, we are captured here. You were tortured and you almost got raped today, and we are probably going to die if it wasn't for Ethan," I say. Kira stands up and faces me.

"He's not like the other Lions, Noah, that's why he's locked up. Don't you think he would've killed us by now if he was like the other Lions?" she asks me.

I sigh loudly. "I guess you're right," I say. She sits down and closes her eyes. "Somehow we need to break him out," she says. I then sit down next to her and she rests her head on my neck. "Just imagine it Noah," she says. "Imagine what?" I ask.

"Once we get out of here, we could go off. We could have adventures together…" she pauses and runs her hands down my back. Her beautiful blinking eyes staring at me. Her mouth curved into a sweet, mysterious smile.

"We could do all sorts of things. We could free the Lion Bloods here, rescue Ethan, and kill some people if we have to," she says. "Mmmmph," I mumble. "We could hunt and have strong weapons. I could have *Bloodshed* in my hands killing everything in sight. Noah we could make this world right again like it once was years ago," she stares at me excitedly."

I would love that," I tell her. "Then let's do this Noah. We can save this world from crumbling in the girlish hands of Andrew," she says then laughs. I nod and kiss her lips. "Yes, let's do it," I agree with her. She giggles and jumps up and down. "Yes! Thank you, thank you!" she quickly kisses my cheeks.

"Whoa," I say out loud. She laughs. "Imagine it Noah," She whispers in my ear. I smile and look her in the eyes. "Kira you are a great person with great intentions. I don't think I would find another girl with your free spirit. I could just live with you forever," I say. She blushes and hugs me tightly. "Let's free Ethan first ok?" she says. *We always need Ethan for some reason. Well not "we," she needs Ethan.* I nod and she smiles. She yawns loudly and we sit down and she rests her head on my chest. I swallow deeply and feel my body tingle. Kira makes me feel different in a good way, and I like it.

I wrap my arms around her and she sleeps softly on me. I close my eyes and try to sleep.

I am woken up by moaning. I look down at Kira and she's twitching and groaning in her sleep. *That's kind of cute.* I giggle lightly and I stroke her hair. She then yelps loudly and she wakes up. She pants loudly and she crawls away from me and starts crying. "Kira?" I say. "Noah were you touching me in my sleep?" she asks. "All I did was stroke your hair," I admit. "Oh… okay," she says nervously. "Did you have a nightmare?" I ask. "I don't want to talk about it," she says. I try to hold her but she shakes when I touch her. Just then, the door opens up.

"Get up you two!" a guard screams at us. Kira stands up first and I stand up next to her. "King Andrew demanded you two to be in the dining hall immediately," The tall guard says. Kira and I follow the guard and we sit down in the same chairs as yesterday. King Andrew then walks in with a big smile on his face. "You two are going to have fun today!" he exclaims. I squint my eyes then Kira speaks out. "What are we doing?" Kira asks. "We're going to play a little game," he says. "I don't like playing games," Kira says. "Don't worry, it's a fun game," Andrew says.

He takes Kira and I outdoors. We cross over a large, wooden bridge over a massive river that flows around the Kingdom. We walk up a dirt path that lead to the outside world. I turn around and see that the main entrance to the Lion's Kingdom was a large cave. We stop and look at miles and miles of forest in front of us. The sky was perfect and there was a nice breeze that blew my hair in my face. I brush the hair out of my face and look towards Kira. *I don't get it, are they letting us go?*

"Hey what is this?" Kira screams. "Calm down girl this will all be over soon," a voice echoes in the sky. She scoots closer to me and we start walking forward together. I hear a soft rustling in the trees and I grab Kira's hand. She looks over at me curiously. "I'm not taking any chances," I tell her. We both stop when we see a mutant Lion slowly walking towards us. I stand in front of Kira and she holds my arm.

"Kira, I want you to run," I say to her.

"No way! I'm not leaving you alone with a Lion!"

"And I'm not letting you fight with a Lion, Kira! Now run!"
I say getting furious.

Kira then climbs up in the tree next to us and I mutate in front of the Lion. He growls at me and I step closer to him and growl back. All of a sudden a knife goes through his thick skull and he growls loudly in pain then falls in front of me. I turn my head and bark at Kira. "Noah look out!" she screams.

Then another Lion bites at my hind leg and Kira screams my name. I whimper and howl in pain. I fight the one Lion as I watch about six more Lions try and shake Kira out of the tree. I howl at her and she mutates. *Kira no!!* She lands on her paws and the Lions back away from her. One of them attacks her and she roars and fights back ferociously. She sinks her fangs into one of them then claws the others. The blood of the first Lion stains her white fur.

I watch Kira carefully as she kills two of them then she falls down to the ground loudly. A big blue dart struck her in the side. I look over and see the same dart in my side. I then suddenly feel very sleepy. The dart says, "Sleeping tranquilizer," on it. I whimper once more and stare at Kira's body. My head gets dizzy and the Lion drags me away. The last the thing I see is Kira's body lying motionless on the ground. Darkness and pain shivers throughout my weak Wolf body.

15 KIRA

"Wake up," A deep, threatening voice echoes around in my head. Blurry faces hang over my body. *What happened to me? Where am I?* A yellow light shines brightly in my face and my eyes stay shut. My body shakes in pain.

"Sit up now sweetheart, we have something to discuss," an angry voice screams at me. I open my eyes while my mind wanders about what happened. "Where am I?" I ask the tall blurry figure next to me.

"You're in the infirmary, where else did you think you were??" The angry voice yells. *That voice sounds familiar.* I look up to him. "Who are you?" I ask softly. "What are you blind, girl??" he screams.

"Um King Andrew sir, she may have some loss of her memory from the past day. The sleeping tranquilizer can do that," A friendly, female voice says to the man. The blurry faces become clearer. *Oh it's King Asshole. What a nice surprise for him to visit me.*

"Oh it's you," I say to the King disappointed. He frowns at me. *Don't worry, I'm not happy to see you either.* I sit up and glance over at the beaten up figure next to me with bruises and cuts all over his body. I study him for a moment and notice that he's not moving at all. "Noah?" I say and grab his arm. *Oh thank god, he has a pulse.* "No, please wake up…" I whisper to him.

"Sweetie he's not dead don't worry, he's just unconscious. The sleeping tranquilizer has a lot of negative effects. You just woke up after sleeping for a day. He will wake up in a few hours. We will take good care of him, I promise," the sweet nurse says. Her voice slightly reminds me of my mother. "Please do take care of him and tell me when he wakes up," I say. "Of course, miss," she replies. *Great. Ethan is wounded in jail; Noah is unconscious; and now King Asshole knows my Blood. He should have just killed me already instead of putting me to sleep for a day.*

"C'mon sweetheart, we are going on a little walk," King Andrew says sternly. *This can't be good.* I kiss my fingers and gently place it on Noah's cheek. "Get well soon," I say.

The King grabs my arm and he drags me out of the room. The nurse protests against him for taking me out of the room, but he threatened to kill her if she spoke out against him again. He takes me towards the small town where the Lions live. It has massive buildings and huts everywhere. However, instead of grass and trees, there is dirt and dust. Small markets and stores are scattered in the streets. Most people here don't look so friendly. The kids bully one another and the women cry louder than the screeching babies. Men curse and spit everywhere. I feel uncomfortable being here. *No wonder Ethan hated living here; this place is horrible. I would have run away too if I lived in this disgusting place.* I look in the center of this poor area and see a tall post with a rope dangling from it.

"Watch this, girl," the King says then points at the post. I watch closely at the podium as a scruffy, old man, who is handcuffed, gets escorted up to the post by two guards. Another man walks up and puts a dusty old bag over his head. The second man then places the rope around the older man's neck. The man then pulls a switch on the side of the post. A platform underneath the handcuffed man flips and the older man starts choking and gagging loudly.

"What are you doing to him?!?" I scream. The King pulls my arms behind my back and I watch as the man chokes loudly and his body twitches violently for a few minutes. Lion's gather around to watch the hanging. His body then went stiff and a tear slid down my face. "Wh-Why did you do that?" I stutter.

"Some people do stuff, say stuff, and even think about stuff that I don't like or agree with. When I catch them talking about it, or if someone tells me, this is their punishment. This is what happens to over-thinkers like you," he tells me. "So you brought me here to kill me is that right? You were waiting for me to wake up from my sleep for a day just to bring me out here and kill me." I say. The King looks down at me with a stern face. "No," he says.

He captures random Bloods, tortures people, kills people for speaking out against him, and his son is a demented pervert who likes to torture people as well. What else do I not know about this great man? The men move the dead body away and I swallow deeply. The King pats my back and guides me over to the small market.

"So, you have been lying to me this whole time," Andrew starts. *Define lying. More like, I am trying to stay alive so I will not tell a King who hates Tiger Bloods that I am one and that I will cause disruption in Bitotem, but yes, lying is one way of putting it.* I look at the somewhat fresh oranges and mangos in the market and say nothing. He groans in frustration.

"I had to lie; otherwise, you would have killed me,"

"Sweetheart, I wouldn't hurt or kill you. You're...special," he laughs. I can hear the lying in his voice. *Oh yes I am so very special for being a giant kitty cat that could destroy the whole world. Why don't you put me behind bars and have kids pet me for a couple gold coins if I am so special?*

"I'm your enemy, and you want me dead."

"I wasn't your enemy until you came here. People pick their friends, boyfriends, lovers, wives, husbands, even enemies. So in all honesty, you *made* me your enemy, sweetheart," he says looking me in the eye.

You were my enemy the minute you started killing and kidnapping innocent Bloods and killing all the Tiger Bloods left in Bitotem. I stay silent. Andrew takes a fresh mango from the market and hands it to me. He tosses the merchant a gold coin and he nods respectfully. "I'm not hungry," I lie. *Oh come on, Kira, he can't poison a mango he just bought, just eat it.*

"Eat, you're going to starve. Look at you, you're already skinny enough," he says pointing at my small stomach.

"I'd rather starve than eat any food from you," I snap.

"Sweetheart, I don't like your attitude. I want you to be more respectful towards me," he says.

"How am I going to be more respectful if you keep destroying my life? You killed my Blood, tricked Noah and I into escaping, which led me to reveal who I am and then you put both of us in sleeping comas!" I yell.

Tiger's Blood

He scrunches up his face and says nothing. I took a bite out of the juicy mango and my mouth tingles with delight. I lick the juices from my lips and take another bite. I wipe my mouth with my sleeve and look up to him.

"My dad would have killed you if he saw you holding me captive," I say.

He then looks down at me and gives me a curvy smile:
"Tell me about your family."

"My mom died when she gave birth to my sister. My mom was an Owl Blood and my dad was a Bear. My sister passed away a few years ago and my dad disappeared around the same time my sister died. I assume he's dead as well; there is nothing really interesting in my family,"

"Your dad…disappeared?" he asks.

"Yeah, he left and never came back. He left me a note, but it's in my backpack and that's somewhere on the surface," I say.

"I'll send one of my Lion's to find your backpack and we will take a look at that note," The King says. I look at him and nod. "Wait, I'm sorry; I just remembered that the note is missing too. My memory is still slowly piecing things together," I say. "Oh well that's too bad," he says in a negative tone. *That's right, it was stolen. Ethan took it when he left Noah and I in the middle of the night.*

"So, Miss White Tiger Blood huh?" he chuckles. *What is with people and thinking a White Tiger Blood is so different from a normal Tiger?* I say nothing and breathe in slowly. He then stops walking for a moment and looks me in the eyes. "You are a beautiful White Tiger, and a great fighter as well," he says. I roll my eyes. *Flattering me won't make me hate you less King Asshole.*

"I do have a question for you King Andrew if you don't mind me asking," I say. "Not at all, what is your question?" he asks. "Many years ago, you set fire to the Tigers territory over on West Bitotem and left every Blood who lived there dead. Why did you do it?" I look up into his eyes and he smiles back at me. "There was a Tiger Blood I knew ever since I could remember. We were close friends until we both discovered our Bloods. After that, we slowly grew

81

apart from each other. On my wedding day, we shared a drink together. Months after the wedding, my wife Lynn gave birth to my son, Jett. The Tiger Blood and I never talked until one day when someone told me very interesting news. The Tiger Blood betrayed me and we started to fight, Blood on Blood. After we fought, I set fire to the Tiger's camp and left on the next boat here with the rest of my Lion Bloods. My wife unfortunately died in the fire."

I take a deep breath in. "So, it was only one Tiger Blood that betrayed you and so your next big thought was to destroy the whole Ambush of Tigers?" I ask. "Yes sweetheart, I destroyed the whole Ambush of Tigers so that I wouldn't have to deal with anymore of their aggressive, backstabbing ways. They are all the same stupid, unpredictable Blood. If I didn't kill them all then I would have been betrayed even more," he protests. "Then why am I still alive exactly?" I question him. "Because I can do whatever I want as King and what I want is for *you* to live a little longer to prove to my Kingdom that Tigers are nothing but divisive and threatening Bloods who will betray you," he snarls. *I'm so flattered that he wants me alive to prove a point.*

"Can I go back to the infirmary? I want to see how Noah's doing," I ask.

"Yes you can, but don't think that I won't kill you. I will when I grow tired of you eventually or if you make me angry somehow," He chuckles then brought me back to the infirmary. *That's not hard to make you angry. All I have to do is speak my mind and you will be instantly against me because I'm a Tiger. I bet that's what that other Tiger Blood did. I bet they said something about Andrew and he somehow found it offensive and responded instantly with violence. Typical Lions.* On my way back, I walk past the prisoners and Ethan winks at me. I force myself to smile, despite all my pain, and I keep walking.

I enter the infirmary and notice that Noah is gone from his bed. The blonde nurse walks in a minute later and I glare over at her. "Excuse me ma'am, where did Noah go?" I ask her. "He woke up about an hour ago, and he went back to his room to rest. He asked if you were alright when he woke up, and I told him you are doing well. You should be resting as well," she says sweetly. "Thank you," I say and head back down to the room with my head thumping loud with every step I take.

16 NOAH

I lie shivering on the ground as I whimper lightly. *The last thing I remember was Kira's body lying motionless. When I woke up, she was gone and that made me nervous. I really hope she is ok.* The door creaks open then slams shut and I flutter my eyes. I breathe heavily and I crawl over to the small body lying in the corner. I wrap my arms around her waist and press my lips against her neck. "Kira, you're ok…" I mumble. I flip over her body slightly and kiss her nose, cheek, and forehead. She looks up at me then squirms over on to her side and I let out a little laugh.

"Oh Kira, if only you knew how much I care about you," I say then kiss her neck. *I'm so glad that she is alive. I was very worried when I woke up and didn't see her beside me. I don't know what I would do if I lost her.* I run my fingers through her curly hair and snake my hands down to her waist. I then tug on her shirt a little bit. *I want to show her how much I love her and how much she means to me.*

"Kira…" I whisper. She groans lightly and flips around to face me. She opens her eyes and stares up at me. I go in to kiss her plump lips, but she resists. I raise an eyebrow at her. She blinks her eyes then looks back at me. I went in for another kiss and her lips graze mine slightly. She then pulls away quickly and closes her eyes. "Sorry Noah, I'm just in a bad mood right now. At least you are okay and that makes me happy," she says. "I'm glad you're okay too. Can I help cheer you up in any way?" I ask. "You can try," she says. I go in again and kiss her cheek.

She kisses my cheek lightly, then my lips. I kiss her back passionately then sneak down to her neck and lightly peck her. She lets out a breath of air as my hands sneak down to her waist. She sits up and looks at me deeply. I take off my shirt first, then I help her with hers. We continue kissing as she begins to shake. I stop and look at her worrying face.

"Let me love you," I whisper. "I promise I would never hurt you Kira."

She glares back into my eyes and bites her lip slightly. I kiss her neck while pulling her jeans down. She moans as I slip off my shorts. I stare at her beautiful body in awe for a second before she covers herself up with her hands, embarrassed. I rub my thumb against her cheek and lift her chin up to look at me.

"Don't be scared, I won't hurt you, but if you want me to stop just say it."

She lets out a relieved sigh then nods. I tell her to lie on her back and she does slowly. I climb on top of her and adjust myself. She looks sadly into my eyes. "Don't worry little Tiger, just relax," I whisper in her ear. I can tell she is nervous. *I love you so much Kira.* I want to say. I kiss her softly and she calms down.

I slowly enter myself in her and she immediately closes her eyes. I move my hips at a slow pace to match up with her. She starts moaning softly and I start going faster. Her moaning gets a little louder and I kiss her neck lightly. We went on for about an hour or so, when I reach my peak and moan softly.

"Kira," I moan lightly.

"Ethan," she replies.

What? Why is she thinking about Ethan right now? I'm the one who has been by her side. I'm the one who has kept her secret. I didn't run off in the middle of the night and leave her like Ethan did. I even helped her find Ethan after he disappeared! Why the fuck does she love Ethan? He has done nothing but got us into trouble. What does she see in him? Doesn't she see that I love and care about her? If it wasn't for Ethan we could be making love underneath the stars and not in a cold dark room as prisoners.

I stop moving and she covers her mouth looking up at me with an embarrassed face.

"You love Ethan," I say softly hiding my anger. Her eyes start tearing up and her face turns red.

"I-I'm so sorry I didn't mean…"

"Kira, don't worry it's okay," I say and climb off of her. *I should've never thought of doing this. I knew she liked Ethan, but I didn't think she liked him that much.* I brush my fingers against her cheek and wipe away a tear. "I want you to remember something," I say. She nods and sits up.

"Real love can last a lifetime. Love is forever, but you just have to know when you find it. If you think that it's Ethan, then I won't get in your way," I fake a smile at her so she won't notice my pain. She nods then kisses my forehead. Her body trembles underneath mine. "Thank you for always being there for me, and thank you for understanding," she says. I kiss her lips one last time.

"I just want to see you happy and safe," I tell her. She smiles then thanks me again. She wraps herself into my body and I smile. *For all I know this will be the last time that we will sleep together like this. I will always be by her side, but as a loyal friend.*

"Wake up you two and come here," A deep voice startles me. I open my eyes and tap Kira on the shoulder. The guard leads us out. We both walk out the door and down the hallway when we stop.

"Both of you close your eyes, because I have a surprise for you," the King says excitedly.

I close my eyes and hear the screech of metal clanging. *What's going on?* I hear a loud *swoosh* of a blade and I react quickly. I jump up then fall to the ground. I open my eyes and Kira takes a step back. A young man has a shiny sword and he tried to strike us. Kira helps me up and I stand in front of her.

"You're trying to kill us…" Kira pauses then look down at the shiny weapon. "With *my* sword?!?!? My *Bloodshed*!!" she yells. The King steps forward. "Sweetheart I-"

"No, stop this bullshit right now," she interrupts. "My name is Kira, not "girl" or "sweetheart" It's Kira," she hisses at him. The King stares at her frightened. I stand up and I could hear her growl deeply. She trips the man holding her sword and she picks it up and held it to the throat of the King.

"I just wanted peace between us…" he croaks out. "Yeah right, I'm smarter than you think I am. I can tell when someone is lying. I know what you did to my Blood, Andrew!!" she screams. I try to pull Kira away from him, but she wiggles out of my grasp. "You wouldn't strike me…" he chokes out.

Kira then raises *Bloodshed*, but then is tackled by two guards. I am also grabbed by guards. "You should not have done that girl," he growls at her. "You're going to die one way or the other…" she growls and mutates. She scratches his chest when one of the guards holds a small, electric box and shocks her. "Kira!!" I scream as the guards take me away. I get thrown into a room brighter than our last room and they put chains on me. Kira's body comes in slowly after mine.

They chain her up next to me and I pet her white fur lightly. *Oh Kira, what have you done? Now we have a higher chance of getting killed.* She then wakes up and the King storms in angrily. "I wouldn't have had to do that if you had just cooperated," Andrew snaps. Kira roars ferociously at him.

"Shut up, I'm done with you, both of you! Instead of killing you, I'll just let you rot and die slowly," he says then walks out the room. The door seals shut and Kira slowly mutates back. "Kira, next time we are in a situation like this we need to think before acting," I tell her. She ignores me. "Noah, I'm a Tiger. We react quickly to bullshit, or at least *I* do. I don't know how a Tiger is supposed to act like," she grumbles.

"Gah, I'm so mad!!!" she says pacing the floor, her chains dangling from her arms. I then grab her small face with my hands and look directly at her. "Listen to me Kira, if we are going to get out of here alive then we need to focus okay?" I say sternly. She nods and I give her a hug. "He tried to kill us and he took *Bloodshed*," she says grumpily. "I know we will get her back," I assure her. The door opens again and the King walks in again. "Where did you get that sword?" he asks. "From one of your best Lions in this shitty

Kingdom, Ethan. The one who is locked up for being different. The one who is actually doing right in this Kingdom better than you ever have done in your entire life," she says to his face.

"Great, then you and Noah can watch him hang tomorrow at dawn," he chuckles. "Or vice versa. I could watch *you* die tomorrow," Kira smiles. He then punches Kira in the nose, wipes his fist off on his shirt, then slams the door loudly. I take of my shirt quickly and I raise Kira's head.

"Here, apply pressure to it," I say and she groans in pain as blood trickles down her chin. She takes off my shirt and almost faints. "Damn, he hit you really hard. Let me take care of you," I say to her. "No I can take care of myself," she groans. "Kira, if you found the Kingdom on your own you would probably be dead already. I hate to say it, but maybe you are right about Ethan. King Andrew probably locked him up because he was trying to help you. He probably hasn't killed you yet because you are the last Tiger in Bitotem. You need to prove to him that Tigers are good Bloods just like everyone else. Prove to him what you proved to me, which is that Tigers are brave, noble, smart, and wonderful Bloods that can change this world."

Kira smiles and sniffles. "I don't know how to do that Noah. Andrew already thinks I'm nothing but a quick-tempered brute," she says. I sit down next to her and rub my hands together. "When I first heard about the fire the Tiger Bloods died in, I was four. I didn't know much about the Tigers. My parents told me that Tigers are nothing but quick-tempered and brutal killers like you said. When I got older, I realized that any Blood can be quick-tempered and brutal. Even I can be quick-tempered. I was when you first jumped down in that hole and didn't listen to me. I just didn't want you to do something stupid. I realized that your curiosity is who you are and I can't change that. I can't change that you are a Tiger Blood, but I can help guide you in the right direction," I say.

Kira cries and rests her head on my shoulder. "It's hard being a Blood that everyone wants to kill or protect. Everyone expects things from you. It's really hard for me to try and please everyone without snapping. I don't want to die Noah. I want to explore Bitotem and go on adventures without worrying of dying every night. I like Ethan because honestly, he's more of a Tiger to me than a Lion. He makes me feel like I'm not the only Tiger left. Of course, you give me more support than I expected, but Ethan just reminds me of myself. I'm sorry. I shouldn't be talking about Ethan like this to you," she says. I smile. "No it's okay Kira, this is what I wanted. I wanted you to take off that Tiger mask and unleash your feelings," I say.

She smiles while tears run down her puffy, red cheeks. "Would it help you if I cried with you? I'm a good cryer," I joke around. She laughs then wipes her face. "No, but can I lay down on you and rest?" she asks. "Of course," I say and she lays her head down and looks up into my eyes. I stroke her hair smoothly and hum a song. About an hour later, most of her bleeding stops and she gives me back my shirt. I sat there shirtless with Kira's head in my lap. "I might not be your boyfriend, but that doesn't mean I don't care about you. I'll always be there for you Kira," I say smiling down at her. "You're a great friend Noah," she mumbles. I smile widely and kiss her soft forehead as she falls asleep in my lap. She is deaf to the sound of my heart breaking.

17 ETHAN

I sit on the cold ground motionless. Bloodstains paint my jail cell everywhere and make it more colorful. *I hate the color red. It looks so threatening and lively. It's like something always is going on. Why can't the world be happy like the color blue? All I see is red, brown, and grey.* I slowly inhale as I change positions on my bed. I've been feeling sick and hurt and just awful. I feel like I could die any second now. I pull up my shirt and gaze at the wound on my chest. Looks like a scratch now, like nothing happened. Wounds heal faster when you're a Blood. It's only been a week or two and it's almost healed up completely.

I look up at the ceiling and slowly breathe in and out as I think to myself. I remember the day when I first discovered my Blood. It was last year on my sixteenth birthday. Chase gave me a new sword as a present and the bakers made me my favorite dessert, custard pie. Chase and I were having a picnic outside the Kingdom when my brother Jett walked towards us drunkenly stumbling. I remember him saying, "Happy birthday to the unknown Prince." I just ignored him and he laughed. He told me, "at least I was wanted. Dad wanted a good heir and I was born luckily with his smarts. You were obviously a mistake." After he said that, something snapped inside me.

I was so angry that I mutated into a Lion and attacked my brother. I clawed at him and roared so loud that the whole Kingdom could hear me. Chase stood in front of me and stopped me before I could kill my brother. I left a scar on my brother's face that healed up later in a month. I can still feel the frustration I had on that day. The year after on my seventeenth birthday, I planned to leave the Kingdom. I told my dad that for my birthday I wanted to spend a little while hunting and he let me, surprisingly. I'm glad that he did, because I met Kira a couple months after I left.

I sit up and look outside my cell. I hold Kira's note in my hand and read it over again. It looks like my father's handwriting since it is so sloppy, or maybe one of his guards. That symbol is definitely the symbol for the Lion Bloods. I remember because my dad told me that mom designed the original symbol but he didn't like it and changed it. I don't remember him sending out fake letters four years ago though. *I don't remember the last meal I had, why would I remember something that happened four years ago?* If he somehow sent this to Kira I'm going to kill him.

Kira....what has the devil of my dad done to you? I just hope she's okay. She's wonderful, amazing, and intelligent. I can see why Noah likes her. I would do anything to make her mine. I would give her anything she desires starting with making peace in the world like she wants, and I wish I could give her even more than that. We could be married and she could be my Princess, or maybe Queen one day. I want to be always be by her side, show her love, be her balance. She comes from a broken family. I'm royalty, but I'm not being treated like the Prince I am. I would treat her like a queen, even if I can't marry her.

I wish my mom were still alive. I bet if she was, she wouldn't have my dad treats me the way that he does. Everything is all about Jett in my family. He is the heir when my dad is gone. Then after Jett, it's going to be whatever stupid child he produces. *You shouldn't say that about your future niece or nephew. Who knows, maybe they might be like me. Jett might not even want to have kids and I could possibly be next for the Kingdom. He's not the type of person to get married and have kids. He's good at one thing, which is showing off at being a Prince. All he does is mess around.* I get nothing; I'm the Prince that people don't even acknowledge. I'm the Prince who gets nothing. Well, that's not entirely true, I do get one thing. A fantastic woman by my side, and I can't wait to see her.

"IDIOT!!!!" My raging father screams as he storms angrily into my cell.

"What are you talking abo-" he cuts me off with a hard slap to the face. He picks me up by my bloody shirt and brought his face red with anger so close to me that I could smell the steak and potatoes he had for lunch. "You are not *only* a traitor, but you gave a weapon to an outsider?? A *Tiger Blood* for that matter???" The anger in his voice makes me shiver. *Is it treason for having different opinions than you? If that's true then half the Kingdom would be dead by now.* He drops me hardly on the floor and I scurry to the corner. "I was...just trying...to help her," I breathe out slowly.

Tiger's Blood

He punches me once more in the jaw. I rub my face with my hands and look up into his soulless eyes. "You do not give a Tiger Blood a sword! Tiger Bloods are ruthless monsters who have interfered in my life way too much. They only care about change, and peace and making me look like a fool. I would kill your precious little Tiger right now if I could but I can't," he spits out. I grit my teeth and stand up quickly.

"Why? Because you know that she could kill your ass any minute now? Or is it that our brave King Andrew is scared of a teenage Tiger Blood who could ruin his plans to conquer the world? You know if you weren't such an asshole all the time Kira would have had no intention to come here in the first place," I snap at him. He pushes me against the wall and growls ferociously in my ear.

"You better say your prayers 'cause tomorrow morning you're going to breathe your last breath in the dead air of this world," he says. I stare at him intently. "And don't worry, I'll make sure that girl you admire so much gets a front row seat at your hanging," he says. I inhale sharply and spit on his shoes. He snarls at me then walks out of the room. "Fucking bastard..." I whisper under my breath. *I don't understand why he hates the Tiger Bloods so much. I see nothing wrong with Kira.*

I take Kira's note out of my pocket and rip it up. I watch as the pieces float to the ground, while one piece lands on me. It shows the symbol of the Lions. I growl fiercely and rip it in half. The paper cuts my finger deeply and it starts to sting. I suck on my finger to make the pain go away.

Why did I have to be a Lion like my father. I'm nothing like him. We are complete opposites and I'm the same Blood as him. It doesn't make sense that I'm a Lion at all. My mother was a Lion too, but was she as stubborn and greedy as my father? If she was then my father wouldn't have killed her in the first place. If she was like my father, then I wouldn't have been like this. He must have killed her because she was like me and that's why he has despised me all these years. If only I could talk to my mother. Maybe she would give me the answers that I need.

I climb up on my uncomfortable bed and look up at the ceiling. Now I just wait until tomorrow where I'll be hanged in front of the whole Kingdom. Kira will be there watching me die, fantastic. *Well, we never know. She could have escaped from here already and is planning on getting me out of here too. What I've learned is that you don't underestimate Kira. She knows what to do, and she's smart.* I breathe in and out listening closely to my breathing. *I've never really focused on listening to my breathing before. It's somewhat peaceful.* If I die tomorrow, please make it quick so Kira doesn't have to watch me suffer. I'll follow her in the afterlife and always make sure she is alright. Dead or alive, I'm going to take care of her.

18 KIRA

I don't know how this is going to work out at all. For once, I am having doubts. Tiger's aren't supposed to have doubts. They are supposed to be confident, focused, and independent. I'm usually doubtful, scared, and dependent on others. *How am I a Tiger's Blood again? I am the complete opposite. I'm weak and I make stupid mistakes. I feel like I have to live up to my Tiger's Blood name.* Noah and I have to escape and cut the rope on that hanging post to save Ethan, but how? We need someone on the inside to help us.

"Beep. Beep. Beep," I turn towards the door to see a dark figure standing in the doorway. I blink my eyes and see his finger go to his lip. He walks in slowly and unchains my arms with a key. He motions his hands telling me to follow him. Without hesitation I walk towards him slowly, leaving Noah asleep on the floor. *I'm sorry Noah, but this guy is helping me escape. I'll come back for you. Sweet dreams.* I approach the unfamiliar face and he pushes buttons on the metal box and the door closes behind me.

He stands a foot taller than me with dirty blonde hair on his scalp. He greets me with a friendly smile and his blue eyes glimmer at me. He wears a dirty brown apron around his waist and his hands are covered with black gloves. He quickly pulls me to the side as a Lion guard walks past us. "Hello my lady, my name's Chase," he says slightly over a whisper. "Hi…" I say nervously. He chuckles. "You must be Kira," he says. "How do you know who I am?" I ask curiously. "Well, I don't normally listen to rumors, but apparently you are a special Blood," he says.

"Yes, I'm a Tiger's Blood," I confirm. *Great, now rumors are spreading about my existence. Just great.* "What? No that's not what I meant. I meant you are a *White* Tiger's Blood. Those are extremely rare. Actually, I think you may be the only one existing. *That's* what got me so excited," Chase exclaims.

Again with the White Tiger. What is so special about it? It's just a color. I raise my eyebrows and chuckle a little bit.

"You know I've never thought of that. Being a White Tiger Blood instead of Orange never really bothered me. I don't know why everyone is so intrigued about it," I confess. "I'm glad that it doesn't bother you. Most people who have something unique about them normally like to gloat. It's just unusual that Orange is the normal color for a Tiger Blood, and you turned out White. It's like if we had a Purple Lion or a Blue Bat Blood. It's funny how the most unusual things can be so fascinating," he says. "Hahaha, Blue Bat Blood. That's fun to say," I say.

"Try saying that five times really fast without messing up," I bet him. "Blue Bat Blood. Blue Bat Blood. Blue Blat Blood. Dang it I messed up," Chase laughs. I laugh along with him. Chase then stops laughing and he tells me to be quiet. I nod at him and he starts walking to the right. I walk to the left side of him and follow swiftly.

"You are probably wondering why I let you out of your holding cell," he says. "Yes I am," I reply. "Well, just keep following me. It's like one in the morning. No one knows you're out. King Andrew reduces the number of guards at night, which is a stupid idea on his part," he says. "That is stupid. That's probably how Noah and I got in here so easily," I laugh. We keep walking down a narrow hallway and turn left into a gigantic room filled with weapons of all kinds. Older weapons, small weapons, even weapons I've never seen before. I just stand there in awe. *Is it my birthday already for me?* "I'm an Eagle's Blood by the way. I work as the Lion's head weapon designer and creator," he explains.

"But, you're like fifteen!" I exclaim. "Seventeen, and that doesn't mean I can't design weapons. Age doesn't matter as long as you know what you're doing and you do it well. Believe it or not I started designing most of these when I was eight," he smirks. "Very impressive," I nod and examine the weapons around me. "And how old are you miss Tiger's Blood? Twelve?" he says humorously. "Very funny, I turn seventeen soon. My birthday is in the coldest season. The last month of the year. I wish I had a calendar to look at. I've been traveling for so many years now that I lost track of the dates," I tell him.

"I have one over here, here you go," he bends over and hands me a large calendar. "It should be the cold season now. The snow has started to fall already outside the Kingdom," he shrugs. "Huh, my birthday could have passed and I wouldn't even know it. What day is it today?" I ask. "I believe December 2nd," he says. "Oh my birthday's next week on December 12th. Sweet, I'll be seventeen," I exclaim. "I would say happy birthday but I don't think you'll have one if you're living here," Chase says.

We sit in silence for a moment before Chase walks out the door again. "Can you help me carry this barrel Kira?" Chase asks. "Yes," I say and help him pick up this brown barrel with what feels like tools inside it. I follow him until we stop at the end of the hallway. A sign read, "Non-Lion Bloods," with an arrow pointing downwards. "Come on, this is where I live besides the shop," he explains and we walk together down the stairs. We walk on the worn down stairs and at the end was a large door with an electric lock on it. Chase punched in a bunch of numbers and the door slowly opens up. A stream of barely lit lanterns flows down a line of ginormous caves of rock and dirt. Each cave has different symbols above them. We put the barrel in the middle of the area and Chase thanks me.

"This is where the Non-Lion Bloods live and the Bloods who are captured by the King's rule. If different Bloods aren't useful for the King in any way, then they go here," Chase explains. "What are those symbols?" I ask pointing above the cave. "Those are the symbols of the different Bloods who are here. Over there to the left are all Bird Bloods, but since I work here, and King Andrew somehow trusts me, I get my own cave with my family," he says. "That's nice," I say and he nods. "Hey Chase, how did you discover your Eagle Blood?" I ask curiously,

"Hah, well it's nothing special. I was here in the Kingdom and I hadn't made a new weapon in weeks. I was stuck and I couldn't think of an idea. I went on a walk one day and it was really windy. I climbed up a tree, when the wind knocked me off the branch. I screamed and I was afraid, when I opened my eyes I was soaring through the air as an Eagle. I flew around and glided through the air. I looked at the beautiful scenery and I hunted small animals. I was so inspired by my flight that I created the bow and arrow, which is my favorite weapon," he says. "That's really cool story!" I smile. "Thanks, you'll have to tell me the story on how you discovered your Tiger's Blood one day," he says. "If I somehow live in the next two weeks, I'll be happy to tell you," I laugh. He laughs along with me.

"Alright what's with the barrel of tools?" I ask. He takes the small bag of tools out and underneath was piles of food. "Supper!" Chase screams and walks away from the barrel. Multiple Bloods run towards the barrel and take food from it. "King Andrew lets me eat full meals since I work for him, so I go to the buffet three times a day and get enough food to fill this barrel. Since I don't eat much, I bring the barrel here for the poor Bloods who live with me down here," he says. "That's awesome," I say and smile. He leads me to his cave with a tiny lantern shimmering above it. I look around and see nothing but dust and two large blankets. A little body shivers in the corner. "This is Claire, my little sister," he says and pulls the blanket over so I can see her face.

My heart sinks down into my stomach when I see her. Short, straight hair runs down her neck. Her miserable eyes blink at me. Her skin was thin enough for me to see her bones. When Chase walks over to her, she runs into his lap. He strokes her hair as she shakes violently. I could see my baby sister's face when I stare at her. She sniffles lightly as I brush my thumb across her cheek, wiping the tear from her eye as I hold in my tears. "I'm so sorry that you guys have to stay here," I say. Chase looks in my eyes hopingly. He kisses his sister on the cheek then walks out of the cave with me.

"I will get you guys out of this hell hole as soon as I can. I'm going to need your help though," I say to Chase. "What do you need my help for?" he asks. "Do you know a Lion named Ethan?" I ask. He smiles at that name. "Yes, my best friend. He's a great Lion, unlike the rest of them. He is being hanged in a day or two," he says. "No…he won't," I say softly and smile. He looks at me strangely. "That hanging machine is just rope right?" I ask. He nods. "Rope can be cut. All I need are some sharp knives," I say. "No, you won't be able to do it when he is getting hanged. If we cut it off earlier it would be useless, Andrew can easily get more rope within minutes. Let me get to the noose early and loosen some threads so it won't hurt Ethan while he's being hanged, but I'll need a distraction," Chase says.

"That's where I'll come in. You already helped me escape from my cell. All I need to do is find a good hiding place and King Asshole will know that I'm missing. He will have his guards search for me then you can loosen the rope before he even gets there," I say. "Smart, but where are you going to hide?" he asks. "I'm a Tiger, I'll figure that out," I say. "I'll help you with that, I know my way around this place," he says. "Sweet," I say. "Awesome. Let me show you around here," Chase offers. I nod and he leads the way.

"So this is where all the Non Lion Bloods live?" I ask. "Yes, since I work for the King I get special privileges. I get all the passwords to the Kingdom and extra meals like I said before. I knew your cell lock because since King Andrew has no use for the prisoners, I have them help me model and test my weapons and tools. A Blood is a Blood to me, no matter who they are or what they have done in the past," he says. "I like your thinking and I agree with you too. A Blood is a Blood. We are all equal."

He takes me on a nice tour of all the different caves with different Bloods in them. There are Snakes, Cheetahs, and Owls like my mother. There are so many unique Bloods like Hawks, Coyotes, Bats, and Horses. It is so interesting to meet new Bloods.

"Over here are Fox Bloods," he points to the right. "Have you met any Blue Bat Bloods down here?" I ask jokingly. "No, but if you find one let me know," he laughs. "Are you the only Eagle Blood around here?" I ask. "Yeah, I haven't met any other Eagle Bloods besides my dad. My mother was a Falcon. When I started making weapons, King Andrew told my parents that he was going to take me to the Kingdom and put me in charge of weaponry. My parents fought with him about that, but Andrew just said he could do what he wanted since he is King. I told him I wouldn't go without my little sister, so he took us here. I never saw my parents again. I don't know if they are dead or alive. It probably would have been better if I left Claire with my parents. They would have taken care of her better," he says.

"Who knows, maybe Claire could discover who she is and she could be an Eagle Blood as well," I say positively. "Well *if* she discovers it," he pauses. "What do you mean if?" I ask. "She's really sick. I don't know if she will make it in a few weeks," he says softly. I swallow deeply. *I lost my little sister, I would be upset if you lost yours too. Especially in the condition that she is in, its horrible. I would rather put Claire out of her misery than watch her slowly die like that. I guess that's up for Chase to decide.*

"I'll help you," I say determined. "I'll help all of you living down here, whether it takes me a week or a year, I'll help," Chase smiles at me. "How are you going to help?" he asks. "I don't know but I won't stop until all of you are treated better than trash," I promise. "You are a really good-hearted person," he says. "Thank you, I just want to make things right. That's the whole reason why I wanted to find the Kingdom, to make it right again," I say. He nods then continues walking.

We walk for about a minute when something catches my eye. A symbol with a familiar animal paw stands out above an open cave. "What Blood is that?" I ask. "Oh those are Bear Bloods. They don't do much but sit there and come out when we get food," he explains. "I'll be back," I say walking over to them. *Maybe they know about what happened to my father.* "Wait Kira, they are really assertive, so I would just leave them alone," Chase says. *Hah, yes they are, I lived with one for twelve years.* "Chase, I'm a fucking Tiger Blood, they can bicker all they want. I would like to talk to them," I say. "Alright, just be careful. Meet me back in my cave when you're done and we will discuss our plans," Chase says.

I walk slowly towards the entrance of the Bears cave. I stand in front of the dimly lit lantern hung next to me and my shadow cast down upon the dozen men in the cave. Two woman sat silently in the back. They all have scowls on their face as I walk closer. *They seem like a friendly bunch.* One of them mutters quietly to another. I get startled when a thirteenth man comes stomping in behind me. I turn to face him and he holds three bruised green apples in his hands. He has a scrawny body with short, black, ruffled hair and angry brown eyes.

"What are you doing in he-" he cut off his sentence when he looks at me with his dark brown eyes in shock with a trembling lip. He drops the apples and he stares at me intently. My eyes widen and I look to the ground and say nothing. *Oh no.* He walks up so close to me that I could feel his warm breath on my head. He brushes his bony fingers across my forehead and pushes a strand of hair out of my face. My cheeks turn bright red. *No…He isn't. Is he?* He let out a sigh and wraps his shivering arms around me. "K-Kira…" he whispers. I swallow nervously and look up to him with a warm tear sliding down my face. "Hi dad…"

19 Noah

I lower my brown nose to the ground and sniff the moist grass. The scent of prey wafts in my direction. I pick up my speed and pounce on the field mouse. I kill the mouse with one crunch and I drop its little body in front of me. The dead meat stares at me intently and I turn my head sideways. The dead prey gets up and walks away. *That's strange. I've never had my food get up and walk away from me.* I follow it curiously when it turns around and Kira's face flashes into my eyes. I whimper and back away when it starts following me. I howl and cry out for Kira when everything turns white.

I wake up panting and coughing intently. I put my hand to my chest and listen to the sound of my heartbeat. *It was just a dream Noah; a weird, fucked up dream.* My sleepy eyes open to a gray room. I look outside the small window and see the sun slightly peeking out behind the fluffy clouds. *Why was Kira a dead mouse in my dream? That doesn't make any sense.* It takes me a second to realize that I'm alone. "Kira?" I whisper. Nothing but my echo replies to me. *Oh no, Kira where did you go?* I quickly stand up and walk towards the door when it suddenly opens on me and I take a couple steps back.

"Get up you two," the grouchy King walks in. He pauses and looks at me for a moment. He looks around me and then behind the door. "Where is she?" he says softly. "I was just wondering the same thing sir," I smile politely trying not to provoke him. He gets closer to me and my smile turns quickly into a frown. "Noah, Where. Is. She??" he says angrily. "I wouldn't know; I've been sleeping all night," I say nervously. He chuckles and looks down at the floor. "Do you know what I do to liars in my Kingdom?" he asks me.

"I'd rather not know, but I *am* telling the truth sir. I have been sleeping," I say truthfully. He holds a cold knife to my throat and I look up into his emotionless eyes. "It's about six in the morning right now Noah. Today is the day where the traitor Ethan gets hanged and I'm not afraid to put a wimpy Wolf Blood next in line. Now tell me where that little bitch Tiger is and we won't have any problems," he snarls. "I am telling the truth. I will say it again if you didn't hear me the first two times: I was sleeping all night. I don't know where she is. I'm just as worried as you sir, now please don't kill me for telling the truth. That would look badly on you if you killed an honest man," I gulp nervously, he takes a step back from me. "Shit…" he grumbles.

"Is there something wrong sir?" I ask. "Yes, there is a raging female Tiger Blood creepin' around here and she will ruin my plans," he explains in a rather sarcastic tone. *I wouldn't say raging, but okay.* I can feel the tension grow in the area between us. "Would you like me to go out and find her?" I suggest. "No, then you and her will run off, what do you think I'm an idiot?" he snaps. *Well, you did let Kira escape and now she is probably helping Ethan escape as well while we are talking.* "Not at all your royal highness,"
I shake my head no and he storms angrily out of the room. I chuckle for a moment then sit down on the grey floor. *I never knew that Kira could cause so much hysteria.*

He doesn't know when to stop. He's got all this power, but he just doesn't know how to balance it out. Now he is going to kill his own Blood for helping Kira and I when he should reward Ethan for bringing him the last Tiger Blood alive. I walk towards the door and place my hand against the cold knob. I twist it and jerk it a little, but it's locked shut. As I turn around to go back, the door beeps three times and I hear people step in. I face the two large guards and one of them nudges me forward. "Come on, we have to get going," the blonde haired gentleman says. I notice a small knife hanging on his belt. I slowly reach over and grab it and put it in my pocket. *Idiot.*

"Where are we going, if I may ask?" I say in a gentle tone trying to hide the knife. "To the Lion's town area, there is a big hanging today. The King requested everybody to be there, even the poor Bloods," the second man says sternly. "Who is getting hanged?" I ask, knowing the answer already. "Ethan Kingsley, the King's son," the first guy says. My heartbeat increases intently. *Ethan is the King's son? Well I guess that makes a little sense. He doesn't look anything like the King though, or act like him at all. Was this his plan? To get Kira and I down here so his dad could kill us? No, if he did then we would be dead already and Ethan wouldn't be in jail for helping us.*

We walk through the Kingdom for about twenty minutes when we finally arrive at the small Lion's town. The guards let me go and I grunt angrily. "You can wander around here, but don't think about leaving. We will be watching you," the second guard tells me. "Alright, thank you for letting me know," I give them a smirk and I examine the town area around me. The town of the Lions looks small, but still lively. The stores are widely populated as well as the center of the town. *Why would he order everyone in the Kingdom to come see him hang his own son? What is he trying to prove?*

A tall wooden spike with a rope dangling from the end of it stands proudly in the center of the town. I scrunch up my nose in disgust as the stench of blood and death floats in the air around me. The people here aren't so great either. They are always angry, which is understandable considering the fact that they are ruled by a wretched King.

No, that wasn't making them angry. Not their King or his perverted son or the way that he rules, they are all under fear. If they rebel, they will all be hanged one by one in their own town for their families to see. If someone catches them even looking at the King awkwardly, they will be beheaded. I not only sense fear in this poor Pride, but also hope. Hope that their once beloved Kingdom will return with a loved ruler. Unfortunately, we are all gathered here to watch the better of the two sons die in front of us.

He may love Kira just as I do, but from the look and the reactions of the crowd I can tell that Ethan is the King that they need, and even though Ethan and I may have our differences, it is my duty as a loyal friend to Kira to do what is right for her. Ethan and Kira are my new pack, and I won't let our pack break apart. I'll help my unlikely friend, even if he hates me or despises me, but he needs my help and I'll always be here for him. I would give my life if that meant pleasing him or Kira. I love her, and Ethan will protect her better than I can. I look to the gloomy sky and close my eyes and prepare for Ethan's hanging in a few hours. *I will save him, if not for Kira, then for the sake of this Kingdom.*

20 KIRA

He stares at me intently with his dark brown eyes that shine brighter than his appearance. His smile gives me a warm welcoming. His dark black, messy hair sits atop his scalp. His body is skinnier than a twig, very bony, and frail. *This isn't possible. How the hell is he alive? He never came back for me.*

"Kira," the word slips off this tongue and sharply stings me. He wraps his cold hands around me and holds my body closer to him. I can hear his faint heartbeat through his small chest, growing louder as he holds me tighter. "I thought you were dead…" I croak out tearing up. "I thought the same with you," he says.

I shake violently in his arms then step away from him and walk out of the cave. I can feel his frown, his eyes glaring at me. "Kira where are you going?" his desperate voice echoes throughout the cave. "I'm leaving," I say below a whisper. "W-Why? Kira no! Come back to me please, I-I've missed you so much. Haven't you missed me?" he cries out. *Yeah of course, I missed the father who treated me like shit and praised my little sister. Yes, I miss the man who didn't even bother to take me with him to bury Lily then never came back for me. The man who left me a note and I went searching for him and he wasn't where he said he was.*

My thoughts rumble through my head like thunder. I turn to face him, but I can barely look at him. "I…I can't be hurt again. You, Lily, and mom all got taken away from me. Now another love of mine is getting taken away," I say angrily. My father's cold hand touches my shoulder. "All of us are going to Ethan's hanging in the morning. The King ordered everyone to be there, even us poor Bloods. He says it's supposed to be a special event," he says. "How did you know it was Ethan?" I ask. "Rumors get around quickly here. They say Ethan left in a rage and he planned on rebelling against King Andrew. He is using a Tiger Blood to do so. They also said he fell in love with this Tiger Blood," he winks at me. I try not to blush, "I hate rumors, especially when they are wrong," I look down angrily. *Is Ethan really in love with me?*

I breathe in deeply and try to calm my rage. "Kira," he starts. "Don't give me a bullshit speech," I blurt out. He holds his tongue for a minute. I look up to his eyes and his lip quivers. "I know I treated you badly when you were little. I'm truly sorry for that. I was attached to Lily all the time," he pauses.

"I said no speeches, I don't want to hear it. You left me alone when I was *twelve*!" I shriek.

"I was kidnapped Kira don't you see that? That night when I went to the hospital with Lily's body the nurses took her from my arms. I knew it was pointless. I just didn't want to lose her, to wake up every day remembering that my youngest daughter was gone and my eldest was scared and confused. After the nurse took her away, I noticed people running out of there screaming. I ran back to look for Lily when a guard knocked me on the ground and forced a knife to my throat. They put a dirty old bag over my head and when they took it off I was in this wretched place. Kira, if I had the choice, I would have run back to protect you from these Lions," he says.

That makes more sense. "Not all of them are as vicious as you think they are," I say defending Ethan. "Yes I know, Ethan the Lion is a strong-hearted young man. When he was little, about twelve or thirteen, he would come in here and give the poor people his leftovers for lunch and all the rejected food every day," he chuckles. *That sounds like Ethan alright.* "I have a question," I say. "Yes, Kira I'll answer anything," he says.

"That note you left. Why did you leave a note for me instead of just coming back for me?" I ask. "When the guards took me hostage, they asked me three questions. What was my name, what Blood am I, and do I have any family back at home, and if so what was their Blood? I told them I had a daughter back home, but she hasn't discovered her Blood. They said they would take care of you, and by that I thought they meant kill you. They told me when they went back to our house, you weren't there, so they left you a note. The note was supposed to make you stay there. They assumed you weren't strong enough to live on your own and they thought you would just die on your own. They didn't see my little girl as a threat, so they moved on and took me back here to the Kingdom," he looks at me and sheds a tear. I look back at him, then look to the floor. He trembles as he holds my body in his arms.

"Kira... I want you to know that I love you and I always have since the day you were born. You had little tiny hands and feet and beautiful brown hair on your small head. I was really scared the day you were born. I didn't know if I was going to be a good father or not. You are my first and only child now, and to see you still here alive and well and...a White Tiger Blood, it warms my heart. I am very proud of you. If your mom was here right now, she would say the same thing. Just look at you, you'll be how old? You'll be seventeen soon. You're a beautiful woman now. If there is anything I can do for you just ask," he kisses my forehead. I smile brightly. "The only thing I need is Ethan alive," I whimper lightly. "We all need Ethan alive," he holds me tightly and kisses my head again. "Go get some rest now," he says. "I won't be sleeping tonight," I chuckle before leaving the cave silently.

I walk back over to Chase's cave and I watch his sister as she sleeps. *She reminds me so much of Lily. It kills me to see a little girl treated like this. I want to just go up and kill Andrew for this. He kidnapped my father and left Lily's body back at the hospital.* I lay down and rest my head on the cold, muddy ground. I gently close my eyes and a shiver runs down my whole body as I start to dream.

The smell of roses and grass wafts into my nose and I open my eyes to a blurry vision of Ethan smiling at me. I stand up and walk over to him. In the distance, I could hear a faint screaming sound. *Probably just some friends that are playing, It's just a dream anyway.* I take Ethan's hand and he grabs it tightly and starts dragging me away.

"Ethan?" my voice is soft, but echoes loudly. "What are you doing?" I ask. "I have to protect you," his voice echoes in a choppy way. I turn around and Noah is trailing quickly behind us as if we are being chased. "Noah hurry!!" Ethan screams while a cloud of darkness follows behind Noah. "Kirrrrraaaaaa

Oh Kirrrrrraaa," the sky echoes at me in a familiar voice. My vision becomes dreary and I feel my body tremble.

"Kira get up, we have to go now," Chase's voice catches my attention. I flutter my eyelids and Chase stands above me. "Get up, we have work to do," Chase says quietly. "Ugh, it's still dark. The sun isn't shining through here yet," I complain. "You want to save Ethan correct?" he gives me a smirk. "Yes I'm sorry for complaining," I sigh. "Then we start early," he says and walks out of the muddy cave.

I rub my eyes and stand up. I follow Chase and we walk all the way to the Lion's town. We use a flashlight to guide our way down the twisted hallways. *Where are all the guards? Shouldn't they be looking for me? They are probably sleeping or something.* Chase and I walk up to the hanging post. "Kira listen to me carefully ok?" Chase whispers. I sleepily nod.

"I'm going to give you three throwing knives. You are going to stand…" he pauses and looks around. Then he spots a tall building and flickers his flashlight three times. "Up there. I will fly down before everyone gets here and attempt to loosen the rope with my beak and if that doesn't work, use your knife *during* Ethan's hanging. We can't do it before because they will just replace the rope. After we free him, we will make a quick getaway," he says. I nod nervously and he gives me a reassuring look. He hands me the three throwing knives and I look down at them and sigh.

"We will save Ethan don't worry," he says and hands me the flashlight. "I know I'm just really nervous," I tell him. "I know. To be honest, I'm nervous too. I don't want my best friend to die and I'm sure you don't either. Go up to the building now and sleep. They will bring Ethan here in about seven hours," he says then he disappears in the darkness. I climb up the side of the building carefully and when I get to the top, I sit down behind a little brick barrier and rest my head against the wall. *Not even the Lions who live here notice that Chase and I snuck in here. Are they purposely letting us go?*

I sit here knee deep in my thoughts. *Seven hours.* Noah is probably scared out of his mind right now worrying about me. Ethan probably can't sleep right now. *Seven hours.* I should be sleeping, but I'm too scared shitless that Ethan might die soon. *Seven hours.* I can't lose another family member. My dad is being treated as nothing more than a rat in the street looking for scraps. *Seven hours.* I just have to do what's right, if I mess up even a little something bad will happen. *Seven hours.* That's what happened to Lily; I was too selfish and greedy to realize that she was dying in front of me. She was the wakeup call that I needed. *Seven hours. Seven hours. Seven long hours I have to wait.*

21 ETHAN

Cold rain drizzles down my skin as I chase Kira through the bright green forest. She giggles in front of me and I slow down, trying to catch my breath. I look up and notice that Kira disappeared. "Kira? Where are you?" I say. I hear nothing but the pitter patter of the rain smacking down on the leaves of the trees. Moments later, I am pushed down and I fall into a huge pit of mud. I push myself up and I wipe the slimy mud off my face.

The sound of Kira's laughter brought a smile to my face. She looks down on me with those beautiful green eyes and smiles. "You think that's funny huh?" I say. She nods and I grab her ankle and drag her down in the mud with me. "How do you like that missy?" I laugh. She sits up and tackles me and we wrestle around in the mud. I end up pinning her down and kissing her forehead. She wipes off the mud from my mouth and kisses my lips. My dream fades away as I slowly wake up.

I lay on the cold, hard ground of my dirty prison cell. Sleeping on the ground is more comfortable than sleeping on the bed they give me. A cool breeze rushes through my body and wakes me instantly and I blink my eyes rapidly. I shuffle around on the ground for a moment when the sound of the rusted door creaking open catches my attention.

"Get up!" says the first guard lifting me up by my waist. The second guard stands behind me and places the handcuffs roughly on my wrists, which leaves a scratch on me. *I'm surprised that they didn't take my bracelet off of me before putting the handcuffs on.* We walk down the stairs and outside towards the Lion's village. They leave the door unlocked behind me to keep letting in people and I take a deep breath. "This is it," I whisper under my breath and the sunlight shines brightly in my face as I walk in the Lion's village.

Tiger's Blood

I can feel the blood rushing quickly through my veins like rabbits running from predators. My breathing becomes heavy and the feeling of my life disappearing is riding on the back of my shoulders. My head thumps loudly as I look at the dangling rope in the center of the town. I look off into the crowd, looking for any sign of Kira or Noah. *They are probably dead already.* I am ready to roll the dice to determine my fate.

The two guards guide me forward. It takes me a minute to realize that my father is following behind me. I look back at him and he gives me a scowl. Through the crowd, people are throwing cans, stale bread, fish, whatever garbage they have to throw at me. An old woman comes up to me and lightly grazes her palm across my cheek, which turns into a harsh slap across my face. She hisses at me like a serpent then spits at my feet.

"Traitor!!" she shrieks. Soon the rest of the crowd starts screaming names.

"Traitor! Villain! Bastard child!"

Their screams sound like screeching birds pecking at the same worm. *The problem is I'm the worm they are pecking at. Will someone just kill me already so I don't have to hear this crowd.* I walk up to the stage and stare at my lovely, friendly kingdom in front of me squawking curses and spitting out swears towards me. Thoughts of Kira runs through my head one last time. *Wherever you are, please be safe.* My father walks to the stage and stands next to me. He claps his hands together and the crowd hums down.

"My people," he begins. "We've had a rough few years, yes, but we have also been successful. We have taken over all of the eastern lands of our gracious world of Bitotem! I have promised peace, and I plan on fulfilling that promise by killing the one who has caused us all this pain for years," he pauses and points to me and gives me a nasty glare. They give him reassuring cheers. *How have I caused pain for years when I only did one crime? Please tell me that father, and if not me, tell your Kingdom.*

"Now I know there are rumors about a Tiger Blood in our Kingdom. There *is* a Tiger Blood roaming among us. My people, do not be alarmed, we have many soldiers searching for her as we speak. If anyone one finds this Tiger Blood, there will be a reward of one thousand gold coins. If they catch her anytime soon, then she will be the next victim to come up here, I promise," he pauses. The crowd looks around with worried faces. I smile to myself. *I knew Kira would somehow escape. She is worth way more than just a thousand gold coins though. How about ten thousand coins?*

"This man is a traitor. He gave the Tiger Blood a weapon and said gruesome comments about our beloved Kingdom. He obviously isn't a true Lion like the rest of us. I bring him here before you for justice in this world," he fades off. A loud screeching sound distracts me from my father's speech and I look up to see an Eagle soaring above. He flaps his wings twice then lands on a tall building. *Is that Chase?*

"Ethan!!" I hear my name from the mumbling crowd. I quickly turn and search for the voice. "Ethan!" I listen carefully and spot the person. A teenager with black hair waves to me. *Noah?* He points up above me and I turn to look at what he is pointing at. He points at the same building that the Eagle is landed on. I look below the Eagle Blood and see a glimpse of a small girl hiding. *Kira?* She glares into my eyes while a tear slid down her cheek. She then bit her lip and disappears behind the wall. *What is Kira doing? She's going to get herself killed.*

My father finishes up his long and dull speech. A dusty bag is put over my head and I take a deep breath. I feel the rope wrap around my neck and my head starts pounding like a hammer. My heart beats louder than the cheering crowd. *This is it. My life is over. I just hope this death will be quick. Noah, please take care of Kira for me. Goodbye everyone, goodbye world, goodbye Kira.*

22 KIRA

Ethan stands there shaking violently as they begin to pull the lever. Noah stands in the middle of the crowd looking up at me. The platform beneath Ethan slips away as Ethan begins choking. My eyes are drowning in tears as I watch Ethan. My legs are shaking, and my head is thumping. My stomach turns and I suddenly feel queasy. My hands are trembling as I hold a knife in my hand, and two more sit at my feet.

"EEEEEEK," Chase loudly screeches behind me signaling me to throw the knife. I quickly get into position and throw my first knife carelessly. I miss and hit the dirt in the ground. I watch someone pick up the knife and hide it. I see the guard behind Ethan who is holding my sword in his own case, and I throw my second knife at him and it slices into his back. I quickly throw my last knife and it slices the rope and lands into the pole. Ethan's body fell to the ground with a loud "THUD." He shakes his head and the sack flies off of him. The crowd stops cheering and King Andrew looks towards Ethan.

"Who did this?" Andrew yells picking up the broken rope. I quickly hide back behind the wall and close my eyes. I slowly breathe in and out and I look back to see Ethan's body still moving around. I sigh in relief and I look at Chase who bobs his small Eagle head up and down at me. I hear Ethan choking and coughing from a distance.

"ENOUGH OF THIS! I am putting an end to this nonsense!" Andrew roars out ferociously. I quickly turn and look down at the stage. Ethan scrambles to get off of the stage while Andrew sends three of his guards somewhere. Chase flies right over me and soars down towards the stage. He flies in circles over Andrew's head and starts scratching and clawing at his face. Andrew swats at the air multiple times until he smacks Chase to the ground. I watch Noah run through the crowd and get towards Ethan.

He free's Ethan from his handcuffs and bracelet and Ethan climbs up onto the stage. The three guards come back and hand over to King Andrew a shiny red axe. One of the guards grabs and pushes Ethan's body on the ground right in front of Andrew. My body trembles as he raises his axe.

"NO!!" I scream loudly exposing myself. Andrew looks up and glares me.

"Great, now your precious girl can watch you die!" he screams to Ethan. He raises his axe when someone from the crowd pushes Ethan out of the way. Andrew lowers his axe upon that person's skull violently and blood gushes out everywhere from the stage to the front row of the crowd. Andrew wipes the blood from his face then steps out of the way. The person's face is shown and I fall to my knees. My stomach lets go and I vomit on the ground. I wipe my mouth with my hand and I put my face in my hands and my body freezes. He isn't a stranger to me. *No, No, No. This can't be happening.*

Ethan stands up and pulls out a knife that was in his pocket. Andrew yanks the bloody axe from the dead body and kicks the dead body off the stage. He then attempts to hit Ethan with the axe. Ethan ducks from the swing of the axe and he quickly stabs King Andrew in the stomach multiple times until he falls off the stage. Ethan hops down from the stage and grabs Andrew by his slick black hair.

"May no one remember your name," he says loud enough for me to hear and sticks the sharp blade between his eyes. Blood runs down his face. The crowd goes ballistic and they run out of the area. Ethan takes his knife out, then climbs off of Andrew and runs towards Noah and Chase. They are all talking to each other when Chase flies up to me.

"Kira!" Noah screams up to me. I just stand there paralyzed staring at the dead body off the stage. I can't breathe after the sight of that. My body becomes numb and I can't hear anything. *What am I going to do? Everyone just left his body there. He needs to be buried properly. I should just let the Kingdom kill me now while there is still pride left in me.* Chase screeches in my ear trying to get my attention. He flaps his wings in my face and nips at my hair. "Kira we need to go!" Noah screams again. I shake my head from my negative talk. *I can't go. Not anymore. Not after that asshole Andrew killed him.*

"KIRA!!" Ethan and Noah scream together loudly interrupting my thoughts. I didn't even realize that Chase mutated behind me.

"Kira we have to go now!" Chase says pushing me forward. I didn't bother moving, my body still feels numb. He keeps pushing me until I slip off of the building. I scream as the wind blows my hair in my face. I crash stomach first into a pile of hay. The rush of the fall made my head dizzy. *I think I'm going to vomit again.* I move my hair out of my face and stick my hands out of the pile of hay. Ethan and Noah yank me up and they brush all of the hay off of me.

"Kira what were you doing? We were waiting for you," Noah says.

"Chase? Why did you push her?" Ethan screams up to him.

"Because we need to leave now and she wasn't moving!!" he screams back. Chase climbs down the side of the building then runs over to us. Noah grabs *Bloodshed* and the case from the dead guard and hands her to me. I slowly wrap the case around my body.

"Kira what is your problem today? You almost blew it," Chase says angrily.

"Chase leave her alone. She almost watched me die for fucks sake, all of you did. I felt petrified when my body fell to the ground," Ethan says.

"Kira what's wrong?" Noah asks. He notices the tears forming in my eyes. I say nothing and point at the dead body that fell off the stage. They all look at the bloody body then back at me clueless of who he was. I sniffle and wipe my nose with my sleeve.

"He saved you," I whisper, wiping away my tears.

"Who saved me?" Ethan asks.

"My father."

23 CHASE

Kira's tears slide down her face. Her cheeks turn red as a rose. *Her father? That old scruffy guy who pushed Ethan out of the way was Kira's father?* Ethan holds his arms out to give her a hug, but she shoves him away bitterly.

"If it wasn't for your kind, I wouldn't have gotten myself into this fucking mess! I would be back home with my father and my little sister Lily. I would be home with my toys and my books to read and I would be safe. I should have never left my house and I should have never trusted a stupid, ignorant Lion who almost got me killed multiple times!" she says sharply. Kira walks into Noah's arms and he glares at Ethan nervously. I could see the frustration in Ethan's eyes.

"Guys we don't have time for fighting right now, let's get our asses out of here before we get them handed to us on a silver platter. You two can resolve this later, we need to go now," I say irritably. Noah nods and I lead the way. We run towards the exit when a cluster of Lions in the Kingdom blocks our path. They all look at Kira anxiously.

"Are you the Tiger Blood who escaped?" a younger girl asks her shyly.

"Yes I am, but I do not mean you guys any harm. I came from the most eastern part of Bitotem to kill your asshole King Andrew. He has told you all lies, he tortures his own kind, and he has killed many innocent Bloods heartlessly, including almost the whole race of Tiger Bloods. He has controlled and ruled your pride for so long in terror. You all should be thankful that this brave Lion Ethan has rid you of your cruel, senseless, and oblivious King. If I were you Lions, I would escape this underground Kingdom and go up and taste the air above the ground. Look at how beautiful our world is without worrying about displeasing a ruthless leader. Live your own lives, meet new Bloods, do something for a change than stay here and live your lives in fear," Kira says.

The Lions look hopeful and confident until Ethan's older brother Jett walks in. "Everybody, settle down please. I, Jett Kingsley, oldest son of the late Andrew Kingsley, hereby take over as King in the Lion's pride. I will fulfill my father's dream of conquering and ruling our land of Bitotem. As my first order of King, I command that the Tiger Blood be executed. She has caused us all this pain and sorrow in our lovely Kingdom. You just listened to her babble on hateful curses on our beloved King Andrew. I find this personally offensive and threatening to our Kingdom and if I hear any more of it from anyone they will be hanged," Jett says.

"Don't fall for his fancy talk Lions, I'm not the one causing you this pain, the Kings are!" Kira screams. "Kira, come on we need to go now," I pull her back. Kira mutates and the Lion's back away in fear. "My people she will not hurt any of you," Ethan says calmly. They all run away horrified by seeing Kira's Tiger Blood. "Noah, come on we have to hurry," Ethan says. He climbs up on Kira's back and Noah follows.

I step in front of Kira and touch her large pink nose, "Kira follow me ok?" I scream. She inhales then gives a deep growl in response and I mutate and fly ahead of her. She follows me through the Kingdom quickly. My black and white feathers float gently off my wings as I glide through the air, watching the Kingdom flee in terror over the Tiger Blood intruding.

They run swiftly throughout the Kingdom as I fly ahead. Kira knocks into the walls and some bricks fall on her, but they keep on proceeding. I use my Eagle sight to watch Kira from above. Noah grabs onto Ethan shoulders trying to keep balance. I don't blame him, Kira runs and leaps very fast, almost faster than me flying. I lead her towards the entrance of the Kingdom. There are multiple guards in the Entrance towers. They fire multiple arrows at us, and one grazes Kira on her face. She growls and shakes it off. "Kira keep going, you're doing great." Ethan encourages her.

We cross the rock bridge over the river that surrounds the Kingdom and I flap my wings quickly and land softly on a rock next to the river. I mutate and

Noah and Ethan hop off of Kira. "Kira drink some water, you need some more energy." Noah scratches her behind her small round ears. Kira grumbles and drinks from the river. Her long pink tongue laps up the water from the clear river. I look off in the distance at the Kingdom. I notice a group of people running out of the entrance. The guards fire arrows at them, but they miss. "Hey guys, look some people must have listened to Kira's speech," Noah points over at the same small group I notice.

"No, those aren't Lions, they are the captured Bloods. I left the door unlocked from the caves under the Kingdom where I live. When Kira and I were planning this escape, I knew that Andrew would be too focused on finding Kira that he wouldn't notice his prisoners escaping. I stopped here because I told them to meet me by the river outside of the Kingdom," I clarify. The captured Bloods run quickly towards us and I greet them. "Chase, thank you for saving us," an older woman holds my hand and kisses it lightly. "It was no problem, thank Kira for helping me rebel against the Kingdom. If it wasn't for her, none of this would have been possible," I point over to the large White Tiger Blood.

She strolls over to us and the Bloods admire her presence. "Thank you so much miss Tiger Blood. We will always be grateful for what you have done for us. If there is anything you need or if you need any help, just give us a loud roar and we will find you," The older woman touches Kira's forehead and Kira grumbles deeply. The group of Bloods quickly leave on the path towards the outside world.

A younger woman walks up and hands me my little sister Claire and leaves with the other Bloods. "Thank you miss," I say. She nods and follows the rest of the Bloods. Claire looks lifeless in my arms. "Damn, I didn't know Claire was growing so much," Ethan says. "She's not growing enough. Look, she's barely holding on," I rub her head gently. She coughs softly and opens her eyes. "Claire look at the pretty Tiger. She saved you. She saved us. She will take care of us," my voice becomes scratchy and a tear slumps down my face.

Kira sniffs Claire lightly. Claire puts her small hand on Kira's nose. "Kitty," she whispers. Kira licks her tiny hand and Claire's eyes shut slowly, passing over. I cry loudly and kiss her forehead mildly. I walk over to the river and gently place her body on top of the water. We watch the currents of the river glide her into her watery grave. Kira gives a soft roar for Claire and Ethan gives me a hug. *I'll miss you little sister. Stay safe in the afterlife.*

24 KIRA

Watching Chase put Claire down the river a few weeks ago makes me think so much about Lily. I should have just given her the medicine she needed before I put her to bed. If it wasn't for me, she would still be alive. *Then she probably would have died anyway because of the Lions. They would have kidnapped the both of us and place us with my father down in those caves underneath the Kingdom.*

If I had the chance to make a proper burial for her and for my now deceased father, I would. If the Kingdom wasn't in turmoil because of me, I would try to change their minds about their society. I know that not all Lions are bad. Even though I wouldn't have gotten into all this chaos if it weren't for Ethan and King Andrew, I'm glad I did. I met Noah, Chase, and Ethan throughout this experience. Who knows, maybe we'll meet others along the way and we might just have a chance to change Bitotem for the better where Bloods of all kinds can live peacefully together.

It still boggles my mind thinking about my parents. An Owl Blood and a Bear Blood living together, having two kids together, and loving each other until they both died. They are completely different from one another. Bears are very assertive, confident, and independent. Dad always set clear boundaries towards me, but was very protective over Lily like she was his territory. Owls, on the other hand, are very wise, decisive, imaginative, patient, and are visualizers. The characteristic both my parents showed and passed to me was courage, and that just shows that any Bloods can get along like my parents.

I walk along slowly for Noah and Ethan since they don't like it when I run fast. They sit upon my back and Ethan scratches behind my ear. Snow flurries lightly in the air as the ground begins to look like a white blanket. Chase walks in front of me sloppily. He stumbles off the path and bumps into a tree. Snow fell on his head and he shook it off. I can tell he is feeling downhearted over Claire. I look through two long rows of trees leading towards a small looking building. I roar softly to Chase and move my head in the direction of the building. He spots it and walks underneath the tunnel of trees. I follow and we stop in front of the small, grey house. Ethan and Noah hop off me and I mutate back.

"Noah, Ethan, come with me and look inside to make sure there isn't anybody here. Kira you sit down and rest since you've been walking the most," Chase says. "You don't have to tell me twice," I giggle. I plop down in the snow and feel the frozen flakes melt on my cheeks. My fingers turn numb and my ears turn red. My nose twitches from the cold and I sniffle. I exhale deeply and watch my breath form a cloud in the sky in front of me. It's something about the cold weather that makes me feel happy and alive. I don't know if it's the snowflakes, the way the trees look like they are shaking from the cold, or the grey skies, but I love being in the cold. I wave my arms and legs against the snow and leave a deep imprint. I am interrupted by a hovering shadow.

"Hey snowflake, ready to come inside?" Noah asks. "I'm enjoying the snow, are you sure there isn't anyone living in there? Any Lion Blood Guards ready to arrest me hiding behind a wall or a couch?" I joke. "Not unless Ethan will arrest you and take you back to the Kingdom." Noah says skeptically. I look up at Noah. "Ethan hasn't done anything to make me question his trust yet."

"Yet? What about when he left us in the middle of the night and we had to search for him for three weeks? What about when we found him sleeping in a tree with a brand new sword for you that he claimed he killed someone to get it? What about all the Lions in the Kingdom who needed him there, but he left and ran off with you? Doesn't any of those seem suspicious to you?" he questions. "Wait back up a moment, what do you mean that all the Lions in the Kingdom need him?" I ask. "I just mean that they could use his type of wisdom for their Kingdom to make it better, but he decided to leave it all behind to run off with you. He ran off with a Tiger Blood against his Kingdom who will do anything to stop the dynasty of the idiotic Lion Bloods from ruling Bitotem."

I stop and think about his words. *Noah does have a point. Ethan has been acting strangely ever since we met.* I look up at the grey sky, then into Noah's eyes and sigh deeply. "I do agree that it's strange that a Lion wants to stop his own Blood from ruling the world. I thought they were all the same dimwitted, snobby creatures. I guess that some Lions are brave and courageous and others are lazy and ignorant. There must be some reason he doesn't want them to do what they do. Maybe he has good intentions like I do. I'll talk to him about it if you want. Don't think so negatively Noah, at least we are all alive and safe right now," I assure him. "For now," he mutters. "Alright let's go inside." I say.

Noah leads me indoors and I find Ethan on the ripped up couch. "Hey guys we have a problem. There's only two rooms upstairs with beds in them and there are four of us," Chase says walking down the stairs. "That's alright, Kira and I can sleep with each other, Noah can take the couch and make sure no one comes in and Chase you can take the spare room," Ethan blurts out, Noah and I glance at each other and he rolls his eyes at me. I look to Ethan. *What if I wanted Noah to sleep with me and you take the night shift Ethan? I still feel shaken up about the hanging.* "Sure whatever that's fine," I mumble.

"It's still early to sleep, Kira want to go hunting with me?" Chase asks. "I would love to kill something right now, what do you normally hunt?" I ask him. We start walking out the door together. "Mice, moles, rats, fish. Any small animal really. I know you kill larger things like deer or moose," he says. "Yeah, but snow just started falling. We'll see what we find in the woods and hunt that," I say. "You're a White Tiger Blood, you'll blend in with the snow. The prey won't even know you're coming," Chase says. He was right. Not even twenty minutes into hunting and I caught three squirrels, two mice, and a rat. I carry my prey between my large Tiger jaws when my mouth begins to water. I haven't eaten a full meal since we left the Kingdom. I have to save this food for Noah and Ethan though. Chase soars above me with two mice in his black talons.

Chase lands in front of me and mutates. "Hey, I called you out here to hunt because I needed to tell you something, well that, and I was getting hungry," he says. I drop my prey on the ground in front of him, mutate and lay down to take a break. "I hope you know that we just started a war in the Kingdom, and now that they have Jett as a ruler it's just going to get worse. We need to figure out a plan to stop Jett. There's only four of us and thousands of them. We need more Bloods on our side. More Bloods like you," he says.

"I'm the only Tiger Blood left Chase, how are we going to find more Bloods like me?" I ask. "You convinced Ethan and Noah and inspired me to rebel against the Kingdom that I worked under for over five years. Why not convince others? We might not be Tigers like you, but that doesn't mean we can't fight along with you," he says. "You're right. We should find more Bloods. Now before we either freeze or die of starvation. Let's go home and cook up this food," I say.

After the four of us eat, I go upstairs and examine the room that I'm sleeping in. I walk inside the closet and find clean clothes. I pick up a sleeveless shirt and a pair of clean torn up blue slacks. I take off my dirty shirt and my undershirt. My breasts instantly become cold in the room. The door swings open and I quickly cover myself. "Kira-oh my gosh I'm so sorry I should've knocked," Ethan quickly shuts the door and I hide in the closet. "It's fine Ethan just give me a minute," I say and fumble around with my shirt.

After I get dressed, I walk out and Ethan stood at the door. "Can I help you?" I ask. "I'm so sorry I didn't mean to make you uncomfortable, I just came up here to sleep," he says. "It's ok. I didn't mind if you saw me. I just found some clean clothes and I thought I would change. Did you want to look to see if there's any clothes that fit you?" I ask. "No thanks I'm good," he says. "Alright," I say climbing in the bed. Ethan crawls under the covers next to me and takes his shirt off.

"I sleep shirtless; I hope you don't mind," he says. "No, that's fine," I say nervously looking at his body. I flip around and face the closet and he holds me from behind. "You look beautiful if it makes you feel better," he whispers. I blush and he starts kissing my neck. His hands slide below my waist. *Noah wouldn't like this.* I flip back to face Ethan and he kisses my lips lightly. I kiss him back slightly and he climbs on top of me. *Stop Kira, Noah loves you. You don't know if you can trust Ethan yet.* I stop kissing him and look at him. "I'm sorry, I'm not ready for this," I say.

121

"Why didn't you just say so. I'm sorry I didn't mean to rush you," he says. He kisses my forehead then climbs off of me. "Get some rest Kira, I won't rush you into anything. You are your own Blood, I'll let you choose whatever you want. Even if you want Noah, I understand," he says. *That doesn't make me feel better. Noah is fine if I want you and you are fine if I want him. I don't like making those decisions. Might as well throw Chase in the mix if you really want me to. Shut up Kira you are insane, go to sleep.*

25 NOAH

The scent of wet grass and blood wafts into my nose as I pad along the path. I follow the stench all the way to a cave far away from my home. My nose is so stuffed up with snow that I can't tell if this is prey or if someone is hurt. A distant female scream pricks my ears up. I pick up the pace and the screaming turns to shrieking cries. I howl loudly to alarm the person that I am near. "Noah! Help me!" She echoes out to me. I look around deeply for her through the dense fog. I step in a pool of dark red blood and follow the trail to a fragile female body. She drips with blood down her legs and thighs and holds something close to her that I could barely see what it was.

"Noah, wake up," a voice from the sky calls out to me. I flutter my eyes open and see Kira sitting next to me on the couch. I stretch my arms up above my head and yawn. "Hey," I say faintly. "Get up, we are heading out soon," she taps my leg and stands up. "We just got here last night, why are we leaving already?" I ask. "Chase told me that the Lions will be on the hunt for us and it's best for us to keep moving. If we stay in one place then it will be easier for them to track us down," she explains. I nod and sit up to face her.

"Where are Chase and Ethan?"

"Out hunting, they wanted to catch some more food before we left."

"Can we talk then?"

"About what?"

I hesitate before I answer. "About us. I know you like Ethan and I respect that. I love what you are willing to do to change our world and that's fantastic. I just hoped that it would be just you and I together, then Ethan and Chase

123

came along and I feel like we are starting to grow apart from each other. I just wanted to ask if there was anything I could do to help our relationship as friends or if I can be of any assistance with you and Ethan," I say. She smiles, then starts to laugh loudly. *This was supposed to be serious, not funny.* She sits down and looks me in the eyes.

"Noah, I like Ethan but I'll always care about you. I wish you had come to me sooner if you thought we were growing apart. I actually thought that we were getting closer. Sure it gets frustrating with the war going on and meeting new Bloods, but I'll always need you. If you want to help me, then stay beside me and fight with me against this war. I know you and Ethan don't like each other, but Ethan is a big part in this just like you and I. We can't fight this war alone, that's why we need more Bloods on our side. I know you will be there for me because you are such a great friend. If you want then we can go hunting together or do something where we can talk privately and have fun, just the two of us," she says.

I hold her hand and she blushes. "I would love that. Just make sure Ethan won't be suspicious about it," I say. "I will, he needs to understand that he's not the only person in my life and that I need my alone time," she winks at me. I stand up and hold my arms out to her. She comes in for a hug and holds me tightly. She gives a quick peck on my cheek then backs away. "Now let's beat those stupid Lions for our friendship," she smiles. "For friendship," I giggle. *I'll take being friends as long as I'm with Kira. I'll protect her and care for her as if she is mine even if she is Ethan's now.*

Moments later, Chase and Ethan come back from hunting. "You ready to go you two?" Chase asks. Kira and I nod and we leave the house and start walking in the deep snow. We travel for a few hours before stopping to rest. Kira and Chase start clearing away the snow so we can build a fire. Kira and I gather wood for the fire while Chase and Ethan build shelter for the four of us. I start the fire and rub my hands together for warmth. Kira walks over and sits next to me. I watch as she drifts off looking into the flames. Chase starts cooking two mice on a stick and I look over at Ethan and he drops his portion of prey on the floor.

"This is all we got today. I would have gotten more if Chase hadn't been so picky on what we hunt. I saw plenty of small birds and their eggs to eat," Ethan says. "I'm sorry, but I would rather not eat my own Blood. You can subtract birds from your diet. It won't kill you not to eat the birds," Chase laughs. "I understand where you come from Chase, but those tiny birds like hummingbirds and robins aren't Bloods like us. They are just regular animals. So why can't we eat them?" Ethan asks him.

"It still feels wrong eating another bird to me whether they are Bloods or not. You wouldn't eat Kira would you? Both of you are large cats. You wouldn't hunt the little stray cats that roam around Bitotem would you?" Chase points out.

Ethan starts laughing "No, I wouldn't hunt the strays, and no I wouldn't eat Kira. Eating the animals are completely different than eating other Bloods. We are normal creatures and they are just animals. We are more advanced than they are. It's not like we can just stop eating the animals. If we stop eating them what are we going to eat?"

"Yeah Chase, every animal and Blood eat different things and that's fine. Bugs eat the grass, birds and fish eat the bugs, and Bloods eat almost everything. It's just one big circle at the end of the day. We can't survive without the other insects and animals," I say.

"Yeah and what do you mean Ethan would eat me? If anything the Tiger eats the Lion first. I would eat all of you in one day if I was a normal animal. Chase for breakfast, Noah for lunch, and then Ethan for my big fat dinner," Kira laughs. "Wouldn't it be weird if we were normal animals?" I ask. "Yeah, I'm glad we are Bloods," Ethan replies.

"Isn't weird how all four of us are different Bloods, but we get along so well?" Kira says.

"I like it actually; the four of us are unique in our own ways, but we all can get along and have similar ideas on a subject like what we are talking about now," Chase says. "I like that too. I've always had problems with the other Lion Bloods in the Kingdom. They just don't understand me or got along with me, and they are the same Blood as me! I always knew I was different, but thankfully Kira showed me that I wasn't alone," Ethan looks over towards Kira and Kira smiles back at him.

"I wonder what it would be like to have another Kira, you know another Tiger," Chase says.

"Why do you need another me? Aren't I good enough?" Kira teases.

"You are actually better than good enough. You are a wonderful and mysterious creature. You are very smart and strong and brave and beautiful. I see now why you are the only Tiger Blood in Bitotem, because you are the most unique person I've ever met. Even if we find another Tiger, hell if we find a hundred other Tiger Bloods they wouldn't compare to someone like you. Nobody compares to you Kira," I say. Kira blushes and Ethan rolls his eyes.

"Yes Kira is amazing and very special we got that Noah, but *because* she is the last Tiger Blood, she will always be in danger of something. Lions, other Bloods, even probably the weak Bloods are begging for her to protect them. I say we keep her away from all of that and make sure we protect her from going extinct," Ethan says.

"Extinct? Why do you say that? You do realize that Bloods can't really go extinct Ethan. Our Bloods are our personalities. A baby somewhere far away from here has the same chance to have a personality of a Tiger or the personality of a Snake or a Fox. Just because I'm a Tiger Blood doesn't mean you should treat me any differently than anyone else. Yes, our Bloods are our personalities, and yes, maybe my personality is unique from others but we are all Bloods. It doesn't matter what Blood we are, what matters is that we are all the same and we need to work together to survive," Kira says.

I look over at Chase and he starts clapping loudly. "And the best speech of the day award goes to Kira! What are you going to do next on your journey?" Chase asks. I laugh and clap along with him jokingly. "Thank you so much for this award. I think what I'm going to do next Chase is relax and take a stroll in our glorious world of Bitotem, maybe befriend a Blood or two, and finally kill Jett and take down the Lion's Kingdom," Kira laughs. We all giggle except for Ethan who just frowns at the ground.

"You ok?" I tap his arm. He just scowls at me and looks away. *Jett is his brother.* *I don't think he likes thinking about killing his brother. I mean he killed his own father just a few weeks ago. I just wonder why he hasn't told Kira that he is related to King Jett and the late King Andrew. Maybe he's scared that Kira might not like him anymore or that Kira might try to kill him if he told her. I wouldn't tell her either if I was in that situation. That would be awkward. That's why I'm not going to tell her. That's Ethan's privacy and I will be a good friend and let him tell Kira when the time is right.*

"I don't know about you guys but I'm getting really sleepy," Kira yawns. "So am I," Chase says. "Let's rest then. Who want's to take the first night duty?" I ask. "I will. I'm not tired," Ethan replies. "Alright sounds good. Goodnight everybody," Kira says sleepily before passing out five minutes later. Chase falls asleep quickly after Kira, which leaves Ethan and I in awkward silence. Snowflakes fell lightly on my head. I move my fingers through my black hair and shake my head to get the flakes out. I then look over to Ethan.

He looks up at the dark grey sky and breathes softly. "Are you ok Ethan? Do you have anything you want to talk about?" I ask politely. "Yeah I'm good. I just feel like we are moving too quickly on all of this. I don't want to go back to the Kingdom right away. I don't want to kill Jett, and I especially don't want Kira to get hurt or killed. Why do you even care about my well being?" He gives me a mean glare.

"Because I consider you somewhat of a friend. Kira cares about you a lot; I care about Kira, so I believe that I should care about the things or people that she cares about as well. It's bigger than that though. Even though I know we don't have the best connection between us doesn't mean that there shouldn't be a connection," I say. Ethan smirks, "I know you're not a bad person Noah. I just don't like that you might be better for Kira than I am. I don't know what she sees in me and I have no idea what I could give her. If I could, I would give her the world and take her up to the highest point in the sky where she belongs," he says. I politely smile at him.
"Get some rest Noah. You deserve it," he says. I nod, and I instantly shut my eyes.

Tiger's Blood

I wake up after three hours of sleep to the sound of a loud thundering noise. I look over to Ethan and he's snoring lightly. *So much for night duty.* The loud snarl alarms me and I carefully look around and listen. I look at Kira and she is sleeping softly. *If Kira's not the one making that sound then who is?* The loud roaring sound echoes through the dark green forest. A little bit of sunlight shines down in the forest. I look up to a tall dark tree with long branches and twigs that stick out to look like a hand. Another loud roar emerges from the distance. The tree shakes slowly left and right as if it was waving to me.

The trees shake violently and the ground below me shakes slightly. Chase sleeps silently and motionless against a mossy log covered in snow. *How are they not hearing that loud roar? It's literally shaking the ground.* Crisp brown leaves fall swiftly around me covering the wet grass. *There's only one Blood I know who makes that thundering roaring noise, and that's a Tiger Blood.*

EPILOGUE

I walk forward slowly, shaking off the dripping cold water from my orange fur. I look out and see nothing but forest and grey skies in the distance. I give a loud roar and watch as the trees shake and the leaves fly off the skinny branches. A snowflake floats gently down and lands on my nose. I snort it off and I turn around and look back towards my companion. She runs quickly to catch up with me then stops halfway. She breathes heavily and coughs deeply. Her dirty blonde hair covers her face until she moves it away with her small hands. Her deep blue eyes look over at me begging for assistance. I mutate and walk over to help her.

"You doing ok?" I ask. She coughs and hacks then looks up at me. "Yeah, I've never traveled that far in my life. That was a rough storm," she replies. "I know, neither have I, but we made it safely and that's what matters," I say. She nods at me then holds her stomach in pain and groans. "Do you want me to hunt this time?" I ask her. "No, I have enough strength to hunt. I don't want to lose you while we are here. Let's hunt together," she says. "Alright sounds good. You go in front of me and I'll follow behind you," I say. She mutates and I watch her spotted grey body walk in front of me. I mutate silently and follow her through the darkness of the forest around us.

Her sandy grey fur covers her whole body. Her black spots dress her fur nicely from her small ears to her bushy tail. *I wish I had spots like her instead of large orange and black stripes. Spots look better to me than stupid stripes.* I watch as her rounded ears prick up. I stop walking and give her a low roar. She gives me a high pitched laugh back and I roll my eyes. *I know you're a Hyena, but that doesn't mean you have to always make that laugh. It gets annoying quickly.* She steps back and nudges me forward with her black nose. I sniff the snowy ground and pick up the scent of the wild boar. *Yes, I love eating those fat boars. They always taste better than the normal pigs.*

I slowly crawl forward and watch the boar eat the wet grass. He snorts and digs his brown snout back into the ground sniffing around. I leap forward and pounce on him. I take my fangs and dig them into his rough skin. He squeals loudly and I kill him quickly in one bite. I listen to Leah laugh behind me and I turn around and drop the dead, brown boar in front of her. She looks at me with her dark, Hyena eyes and I take a large bite out of the stomach. She uses her grey paws and claws into the boar until she finds a bone to eat. She gnaws on it while I eat the tender meat. *This tastes so good. I haven't eaten since we left home. We should have packed more food and water for the trip over here.*

After our meal, Leah and I mutate and look around for a nice spot to rest for the night. We look through the dark snowy forest for a couple minutes and find ourselves a small cave. I "We should find wood to start a fire," Leah points out. "Yeah, let's gather up some branches," I reply. Leah follows behind me and I breathe in and out slowly. *I hope we find what we are looking for. I don't want either of us to get hurt or killed, especially Leah. She's my best friend; I shouldn't have had her come with me. I knew we would be put in danger.* We find a small area of tiny trees and start breaking off the branches.

We gather up enough wood for three fires and begin to walk back towards our cave. All of a sudden, I hear Leah shriek loudly. I turn around quickly and walk to her. "Leah what's wrong?" I ask. She points down at a dead body cloaked in a sheet of snow. I drop the branches in my hands and bend down on my knees. Leah gets down too and helps me brush the snow off of him.

His body is completely frozen and stiff. His eyes are still open which made him look really creepy. The body has a full suit of metal armor with a sword and many other weapons attached to his waist. *Ugh, this guy was a Lion. I hate Lions, well all except one. I'm glad that he's dead. I hope I don't have to meet any living Lions on this trip. They are ignorant and selfish Bloods.*

"Do you think this guy was a knight?" Leah asks me. "No, not a knight, I think he was a guard for the Lion Kingdom. You see all of this armor? Only place who makes armor over here is the Lion's Kingdom. Knights are brave and noble warriors while guards just blindly follow whatever orders they are told," I say. "Maybe that means we are close to where we should be," she says. I nod and take his sword and the rest of his weapons from his body. "Skylar!

Those are his weapons. We can't just steal them from him that's rude," she says. "Oh yeah? What is he going to do with them Leah? Fight off the ghosts around here? Come on be more realistic, a dead man doesn't need weapons," I say.

"Yeah but what do you need weapons for Skylar? You are a Tiger Blood. You don't need anything. You have your strength and your power," Leah says. "Just because I'm a Tiger Blood doesn't mean I'm all strength and power. You can't be strong without being weak," I tell her. "True," she says. I gather up my portion of the branches and Leah grabs hers and we walk back to the slimy cave. We throw our branches in the middle of the cave, and I pull out a match from my pocket, light it up, then throw it into the wood.

I watch the fire rise up so high that it licks the top of the cave. The orange flames burn brighter than my hair. I comb my straight, long, orange hair with my fingers. I stretch out my arms above my head and my legs in front of me. I look over at Leah who gives me a crooked smile. "What are you smiling at?" I ask. "You always look prettier than me no matter what you are doing. It makes me jealous," she laughs. "You are pretty too Leah. You don't have to be jealous. If it makes you feel any better, I'm jealous that you have blue eyes and that I'm stuck with these boring green eyes," I say.

"Don't hate yourself Sky, you are perfect," Leah says. "If I'm so perfect, then why do I keep making mistakes?" I say. "You're not the only one who makes mistakes. Look at me, I lost my backpack with all our clothes in it on the way here and now we are stuck wearing these," she laughs. "Yeah but that was an accident. I kept making stupid mistakes when we were back home. It's hard to fulfill the image of a Tiger Blood to a whole village who's always watching you. I was really surprised when they asked me to take the trip here. I mean I just turned sixteen a couple days ago, I'm way too young to travel on a long journey like this. I'm a little scared about this to be honest," I say.

"Hey, I was even more surprised when you asked me to join you on the trip. I thought for sure that you would have picked a Blood who was stronger than me or a better fighter. I'm just as scared as you are Sky," Leah says. "Leah, you're my best friend. Why wouldn't I pick you?" I say. She blushes and I smile back at her. "I'll admit, I am glad I came here with you. It's so beautiful and mysterious," Leah says. "Yeah, there seems to be a lot more forest here, but that's alright. I love being in the forest," I say.

"Yeah, me too," Leah replies. "Hey, I'm feeling a little tired. Do you mind taking the first night shift?" I ask. "Oh yeah that's fine. I can stay up as late as you want me too," Leah says. "Thanks Leah, I really appreciate it," I say. "No problem," she says. *I miss my mom and dad. I wonder if they miss me too. I wonder what they are doing right now. Probably having fun and exploring new lands and meeting new Bloods. I wonder why they didn't want to come with me on this trip. I don't want to let them down on this mission.* I curl myself up against the walls of the cave and start to dream.

I run throughout the forest chasing after a huge, black creature. He hisses at me as he flies through the air. *What kind of Blood is that? I've never seen that Blood anywhere before. Not even in my dreams.* I stop then I watch it disappear. I look up to the blue sky hoping that he will come back. After five minutes, I give up and start to walk back. My paws start to hurt after chasing the creature and I stop and rest underneath a shady tree.

After my nap, I wake up and hear a screaming woman. I prick up my ears and listen to her. I follow the screaming to another Tiger Blood. The screaming turned out to be Leah. I fight the Tiger Blood roughly when suddenly I am awakened by a voice in the sky. "Come on Skylar get up. We have to start traveling today," Leah says. I yawn and stretch my arms. Leah helps me up and both of us step out of the cave. "The snow must have fallen heavily last night because we almost got snowed in our cave. Luckily, I dug us out of here," Leah says. "Wow, I've never seen it snow like this back home. We are lucky even if we get a few flakes of snow," I say. Leah nods in agreement.

"Did you have another crazy dream last night? You were talking in your sleep again," Leah asks me. "Yes I did, it was scary. You were in danger," I say. "Don't worry Sky, I have you to protect me. I shouldn't be in any danger anytime soon." she says. "There's danger all around us. Even back home we were in danger of other Bloods, storms, even accidents. The dream just scared me because in the dream I had to fight another Tiger Blood. I don't want to hurt my own Blood," I say.

"You shouldn't have too. I know we have to look for that other Tiger Blood somewhere in this area, but I don't think you will have to fight her. Not if we talk to her first at least. Hopefully she will be a nice and reasonable person. What was her name again? I know they told us back at home but I forgot," Leah looks to me. I look back at her. "They said her name is Kira. I don't know who she is, or if she is dangerous, but we have to find her."

ABOUT THE AUTHOR

Elizabeth Morris graduated from Penn Foster Online High School in 2015. She lives in Manassas Virginia. She is the third child in a family of four.